"I'd really like you to be my partner," Ashley said to Richard.

Richard spilled cocoa on himself. "Uh," he said. He looked at me for help.

"I think Mother was expecting Rich to take Fleur," I said.

"Fleur is flying home *before* New Year's Eve," Ashley announced grandly.

I looked at Fleur. "I decided to go to the wedding after all."

"Good," Richard and I said together.

"I thought you asked Kirk," I said to Ashley.

"He can't go," Ashley said quickly. "Will you go with me?" she asked Richard again, keeping her voice light.

I don't know why, but Richard looked at me again. "Are you going?" he asked.

"She's going with Helmut Weiss, so they can discuss transformational grammar." Satisfaction on her smug face.

I sighed. "Helmut is good company, Ashley." Which was more than I could say for her.

"You will go, won't you?" Ashley fluttered the eyelashes. Gag, gag, and throw up.

"Well." Richard recovered himself. "Sure," he said to Ashley. "That'll be fun."

"Oh good," she said. "Have some more cocoa." She poured some from the thermos into his cup. "Do you want more, Kate?"

Pushing my glasses back on my nose, I shook my head. I'd had enough poison for one day.

Praise for

The Unlikely Romance of Kate Bjorkman

★ "Charismatic, lighthearted, and irresistible, Kate Bjorkman narrates her tale of teen romance in the language and conventions of *The Romance Writer's Handbook*. . . . Witty, keen writing, likable characters, and an interesting format form a fast-paced, refreshing book with lots of appeal. . . . Kate is a uniquely strong female protagonist whose reflections on life, love, and people shine through." —*School Library Journal*, Starred

♦ "Plummer has crackerjack timing . . . funny and fast-paced, crammed with witty dialogue. . . . A breathlessly good-natured story." —*Kirkus Reviews*, Pointer

"Readers looking for a funny, light, tongue-in-cheek romance will snap this one up." —*Voice of Youth Advocates*

"The holiday cheer, the appealing protagonist, and the happy ending are sure to evoke the simple pleasures of popcorn and cocoa on a cold winter's day." —*The Horn Book Magazine*

**A *School Library Journal*
Best Book of the Year**

The Unlikely Romance of Kate Bjorkman

LOUISE PLUMMER

LAUREL-LEAF BOOKS

Published by
Dell Laurel-Leaf
an imprint of
Random House Children's Books
a division of Random House, Inc.
New York

ISBN: 0-375-89521-3

RL: 5.8

Reprinted by arrangement with Delacorte Press

Printed in the United States of America

To Kelli Jaggi, who wanted a romance.
This is it, sort of.

Prologue

This is one of those romance novels. You know, that disgusting kind with kisses that last three paragraphs and make you want to put your finger down your throat to induce projectile vomiting. It is one of those books where the hero has a masculine-sounding name that ends in an unvoiced velar plosive, like CHUCK (although that is not my hero's name), and he has sinewy muscles and makes guttural groanings whenever his beloved is near. In romance novels, the heroine has a feminine-sounding name made up of liquid consonants, like FLEUR, and has full, sensuous lips—yearning lips. I think the word "yearning" will appear at least a thousand times in this book. The heroine also has long, silky legs and is a virgin.

The reason I know about romance novels at all is because my best friend, Ashley, was addicted to them last year, our junior year, and insisted I read them too. The trouble with romance novels, I soon discovered, is that they make you feel bad about your life, especially if there is no CHUCK in it, and especially if you don't have long, silky legs and your name ends in an unvoiced dental plosive as mine does (Kate) and very especially if you think you're going to be a virgin for the rest of your life. Mostly, though, romance novels are sappy in the extreme. They read like junior-high-school daydreams. I've never read one that I could really believe. None of them sounds like real life. And I want real life. Even in novels, I want real life.

So what do you do if you have lived a real romance, and it happened at Christmas, and the guy has a masculine-sounding name, Richard, and it ends up that he loves you as much as you love him? I know what I want to do. I want to write a romance novel about it. I want it to end with "they lived happily ever after." And we really have.

Sort of. This all happened last December and it is now the middle of February, so we have lived happily ever after for six weeks. But how many people do you know who are exhilaratingly happy for six weeks? I know it's a record for me.

I want to gloat and bask in this lovely feeling of being in love. And if I do not have long, silky legs and long, blond locks, I do have sensuous, full lips, and if I have not written three-paragraph kisses, I have kissed them.

I'm giving this my best shot. I've got *The Romance Writer's Phrase Book* right next to the word processor in case I'm at a loss for words, as they say. If you are jaded about romance or have PMS or are on the downside of manic depression and can't stand to read about other people's happiness, then get real. This book is not for you.

Chapter One of a romance novel is the chapter where the heroine is described and where she first meets the hero. This is no different. It happened a few days before Christmas. My mother asked me to walk down to Sims Market after dinner and get some cinnamon sticks. She has this hot drink she makes around Christmas called Russian tea—it's filled with cinnamon and cloves and sugar and orange and lemon and stuff—and we guzzle it all through the holidays. It's part of our family tradition, this drink. Anyway, she was almost out of cinnamon sticks. Would I go to Sims?

It was a dark and stormy night. This is the honest-to-god truth. I live in St. Paul, Minnesota, and it was snowing hard—large flakes the size of cotton balls—and it was thundering and flashing lightning off in the distance. If you don't believe it can thunder and snow at the same time, then obviously you haven't lived in Minnesota, the Weather State.

I had covered my six-foot frame in thermal underwear, ski pants, a turtleneck sweater, a down parka with the hood up, mittens with reindeer heads knitted into the tops, and million-dollar snow boots, which my father calls the "fruit boots." I'm not going to apologize for being too tall. I know heroines should be petite, but I'm not. I am six feet tall in my stocking feet. I do have very long legs and nice kneecaps, but I don't know if my legs are particularly silky. In fact, sometimes in winter, when I'm totally covered in clothes all the time, I just skip shaving my legs and see how long the hairs can get. If I want silky legs, I can get them by rubbing Chanel body lotion all over them.

Anyway, the minute I began walking down Folwell Street, I felt glad to be alive. Even before the hero entered, I was pretty happy with my life. I'm not the sulking type. My father, the linguistics professor, had been playing one of the Brandenburg Concertos when I left, and I felt as if the flute music were trapped inside me and that if I opened my mouth, it would trill out into the night air. I caught snowflakes on my tongue the way I used to do when I was ten. The night felt magical. There must have been some foreshadowing in the air.

It's only about six blocks to Sims Market, and pretty soon I was standing in front of the spices, but I couldn't find the cinnamon sticks. I knew the spices were arranged in alphabetical order, but my eyes (which *The Romance Writer's Phrase Book* would describe as "amethyst") skipped from basil to fennel to thyme and back again. There were distractions: the canned music, for one thing. I stood directly under a speaker blaring an orchestral rendition of "Sleigh Ride" and found myself trying to fill in the words, "Just hear those sleigh bells jingling, ring ting tingling too . . ." Then something—weather—something, something—together—basil, fennel, thyme.

The other distraction was Ashley, my best friend, who taught me all there was to know about the romance novel last year, and her boyfriend, Kirk, at the checkout counter making much ado about the dry mistletoe forlornly hung over each checkout aisle. They held the blue plastic shopping basket between them, but Kirk leaned over it, threatening to kiss Ashley in front of clerks and customers alike. Finally he bit her ear, and Ashley's laughter pealed above the canned "Sleigh Ride." When heads turned, Ashley muffled her mouth as if she had committed a grand faux pas. After they set the filled shopping basket on the counter, Kirk took her hand and put it in the pocket of his parka with his own.

The truth is that Ashley is always trying to live her life as if she were the heroine of a romance novel. It never works, though. She rarely lives happily ever after, even for six weeks. But at Christmastime, she and Kirk were hot for each other.

• I tried to concentrate on the spices. Allspice, sweet basil, ground cinnamon—

"Kate!" Ashley flounced down the aisle in front of Kirk, who carried the brown sack of groceries. "I didn't know you were in the store!" Her voice is all dramatic and different when she's with Kirk. I never want to sound different than myself around any guy.

"Oh, hi, you guys." I nodded at Kirk.

"Kirk and I are going to make Christmas cookies together." Ashley slipped her arm through Kirk's.

7

"*You're* going to make them. *I'm* going to eat them."
Kirk wagged his tongue at her.

Ashley leaned into him with her lips. "You'll love cooking. It's a *sensuous* activity."

I was pretty sure from the way Ashley said "sensuous" that the conversation was about more than just baking cookies. I felt as if they were performing for my benefit.

"Sounds like fun," I said. "Save a cookie for me."

Ashley turned Kirk around with a grand sweep of her arm. She was a different person entirely around Kirk. A looney tune.

"See you later," Kirk said, looking back.

He didn't gaze longingly into my amethyst eyes, so he obviously is not the hero in this novel.

At the end of the aisle Ashley shouted back, "Isn't Christmas wonderful?"

What she really meant to say was, Isn't Christmas wonderful when you're going with someone like Kirk?

I forced a laugh for her and waved good-bye. "Have fun, Ash," I called. Like I said, I was happy all the way to Sims Market, but now I felt let down a little. I actually sighed. I was jealous of Ashley and Kirk. A lot jealous, but I did not, as *The Romance Writer's Phrase Book* says, "flounder in an agonizing maelstrom." I'm too buoyant for that.

There weren't any cinnamon sticks on the shelf.

"Mr. Sims." I turned when I smelled the cigarette smoke. Mr. Sims is the last chain-smoker in Minnesota and completely ignores the Clean Air Act. "It's my store,"

8

he says when customers complain. He's known around the neighborhood as "that bastard."

"Do you have any cinnamon sticks in the back? There's none on the shelf."

"If they're not on the shelf, I don't have any," he said, bending over a broken sack of sugar.

I tried not to stare at his thick mustache when he looked up. It always had gunk in it.

"Won't have any until next week." Ashes fell from his cigarette into the open sugar bag.

"But that's after Christmas."

"So?" Mr. Sims lifted the broken sugar bag and blew smoke into my face.

I waved the smoke away. He was so rude. "Merry Christmas, Mr. Sims," I said anyway.

He said something I couldn't hear. Probably "bah humbug." I didn't care. I knew Mr. Sims would become a minor, flat character in my novel.

Outside, it was still a dark and stormy night: it snowed steadily, but the thunder had stopped. I pulled the hood of my parka up and tied it securely under my chin. Most of the stores in "the Park," which is what the one commercial street in this old suburb of St. Paul is called, were still open. Pine bows, red ribbons, and tiny lights decorated the storefronts. That Christmas stuff made me feel festive, and I considered stopping at Bridgeman's for hot chocolate with synthetic whipped cream on top, but then I saw Ashley and Kirk near there.

I crossed with the light and headed home. I can only stand so much hormonal happiness in one evening, especially someone else's. I wondered if Mr. Sims had ever been in love at Christmas. Had he ever been someone's hero? There had been a Mrs. Sims years ago. Who could stand to kiss those nicotine-stained lips?

When I thought about it, climbing the long, sloping hill toward my house, I realized happiness at Christmas is hierarchical. People in love like Ashley and Kirk are the happiest. Next come people like me, who have family and friends, and who, at least, expect to be in love at some future Christmas. Last come people like Mr. Sims—the cantankerous ones—who are never happy, and no amount of external magic, even Christmas magic, can change that.

At the top of the hill I turned the corner. I was on my street now. Through the lighted window I saw the Chamberlain twins dropping toys from their bunk beds in their second-story bedroom. I still think of that house as the Bradshaw house, even though the Bradshaws moved to California years ago. I always pass it with a kind of "upsurge of devouring yearning," as the phrase book says. But I don't think it's necessary to explain why, yet. All you need to know is that on that night I passed the house with an excess of yearning. The holidays bring on those hokey feelings.

Up the street I passed the Midgely house, where Midgely, who is younger than my father, was dying of pancreatic cancer. He had already lived two years longer than the doctors said he would. It had been weeks since I had seen his jaundiced, sunken face. There is nothing in *The Romance Writer's Phrase Book* to help me describe that face. He used to be the tennis coach at the high school, and was also my junior-year English teacher, but had to quit this year because of the cancer. Whenever I think of Midgely now, I think of that Dylan Thomas poem "The Force That Through the Green Fuse Drives the Flower." Midgely was a devoted Dylan Thomas fan. We spent weeks on Dylan Thomas. Was Midgely happy at Christmastime?

Why this grim reflecting in a romance novel? Have I lost control of the writing? Or is it possible that all that yearning for the Bradshaws has turned my brain to Cheerios?

Moving right along: my house had changed since I had been at Sims. More windows were lit, for one thing. Even my bedroom light was on upstairs. Not my doing either. I take after my father that way, economical and practical. My mother and Bjorn leave lights blazing all over the place, but Bjorn was in Palo Alto, two thousand miles away, with his new bride, Trish. Mother had been in the basement when I left, wrapping pots of forced tulips in dark green shiny paper and red ribbon as Christmas gifts for neighbors. Weird. The house looked like a shimmering spaceship freshly landed from some exotic star. And I'm not quoting the phrase book either.

On the porch, brushing the snow from my collar and stomping my boots, I noticed a green Volvo station wagon parked in the driveway. Company. Company changed a house.

Light, warm air and my brother's voice spilled through the widening crack in the front door when I opened it: "We couldn't stand another snowless Christmas this year, and when you said there was already two feet of snow on the ground, we decided to come."

"Is that you, Bjorn Bjorkman?" I yelled, pushing the front door shut with my behind. We collided between the hall and the dining room.

"Boo, it's good to see you," he said. We hugged. He still wore his parka.

"You're here!" was all I could say. I just couldn't believe it. I pulled back to see his face. My glasses were partially fogged, as they always are when I come in from the cold. I pinched his arm. "It's like magic to have you here," I said.

"It took three whole days to drive here; that's not magic." Trish appeared behind his shoulder, and I broke loose to hug my sister-in-law.

"I'm so glad to see you," I said.

"Kate, you look wonderful. I like your new frames."

"Thanks." I know I mentioned my height—six feet—but did I mention the glasses? It's a rhetorical question. I didn't mention them on purpose, because I wanted you to imagine me looking like Cindy Crawford. I have worn glasses since I was three years old, and even when I have cool Giorgio Armani frames, my eyes are magnified about three times their size with these plate-glass lenses. I can't wear contact lenses because I have congenital cataracts. It's a complex condition, but the bottom line is I have to wear glasses or be legally blind. I know this is a disappointment in someone who is supposed to be the romantic heroine of this book, but unless you're one of those really shallow readers, you'll continue.

Bjorn insisted that Trish call me Boo. "That's her name," he said. We had been through all this before and he still wouldn't let go.

"Kate fits her better than Boo," Trish said.

I liked Trish. "No one calls me Boo except Bjorn and his ape friends," I said.

"You mean me?" Richard Bradshaw filled the doorway.

Okay, a flourish of trumpets here. The hero has arrived. And because he was my hero long before I began writing this novel, ever since I can remember, in fact, my face grew hot. He was four years older now, of course, and *shorter* than I remembered, but I wasn't six feet tall four years ago either. His eyes—I need the help of *The Romance Writer's Phrase Book* to describe those eyes:

—*unfathomable in their murky depths?*

No!

—*shades of amber and green?*

Maybe.

—*dark gray-green-flecked eyes?*

I don't know. Maybe.

—*hooded like those of a hawk?*

Absolutely not! The hell with it. They were warm eyes. They were Richard's eyes. I wouldn't care if they were cone-shaped. Richard Bradshaw was standing in the doorway of the dining room. "Hi," I said and stepped forward to shake hands, when I tripped on the edge of the oriental carpet and lurched into him, elbows first. It wasn't a pretty picture. He made a sound like "oomph" because my elbow caught him in the diaphragm. He was too incapacitated for me to fall gracefully into his arms. Instead, I was caught by a drop-dead-beautiful young woman standing at Richard's shoulder.

This would be a better story if I'd just lie, but I want

13

truth in romance. And the truth is that the first time I saw Richard Bradshaw after four years of separation, I knocked the wind out of him and was saved from falling on my face by his girlfriend.

Chapter Two of a romance novel is where the antagonist is introduced. You know, the character who is going to get under the craw of the protagonist, in this case me. The antagonist's job is to try her provoking best to keep the heroine and hero from getting together and providing the reader with a happy ending too quickly. A novel, after all, must have at least a hundred pages of blessed tension. Heroine and hero must be conspired against.

Like I said, *she* was drop-dead beautiful. "Are you hurt?" she asked in a voice that could melt a fifteen-year-old cheese.

I could have sworn she dropped her postvocalic "r." It was subtle.

"Those fruit boots are death in the house," my father said. Had he heard it too? He and Mother were the last to step into the dining room from the kitchen.

"I'm sorry," I muttered. I couldn't help gazing into the young woman's face. The face of an angel.

"She's all right," Bjorn said. "She's used to knocking around in the house."

"Take those boots off, honey," Mother said.

Richard pounded a fist against his chest as if to correct whatever I had injured. "It's nice to see you again, Boo." He used my thirteen-year-old name, but he smiled, and we glanced briefly at each other—our eyes didn't lock or anything—but it was easy to forgive him. Then, as if he had forgotten himself, he said, "Oh, this is my friend *Fleur St. Germaine.*"

I swear to god, that was her real name. Fleur St. Germaine. Would I make up a name like that?

"Richard hasn't been to Minnesota since his folks moved to California," Bjorn said.

I knew that.

"So we invited him to come out with us—besides, his car worked, and ours didn't." Bjorn grinned. "He's in the comp. lit. program too."

I knew that.

"Fleur is in comp. lit. too."

Ducky. I couldn't help staring at her. It was her hair, a mane of California blond, combined with a soft tan and those clear green eyes. "Hi," I said. She was his *friend.* What did that mean exactly? Her beautiful tanned skin made me feel like a marshmallow.

"I'm so glad you all decided to come," my mother said. And I could see that it was true. Her energy level had risen since I'd left earlier. She liked having Bjorn in the house again. "It was going to be such a lonely Christmas with just the three of us."

That was overstating it. The three of us have never been lonely in our lives.

"We really should have called," Trish apologized, "but Bjorn wanted to surprise you."

Fleur pulled her coat tightly around her neck. "If you don't have room in the house, I could stay in a hotel," she offered.

Her diphthong in "house" was a little slow, I thought. A halo of blond wisps floated around her delicate face.

"We both could," Richard cut in. Was there eagerness in his voice or was that my paranoia? In the same hotel room? In the same bed? Possibly. Depressing images of the two of them, loins and limbs entangled, floated through my head.

Bjorn shook his head as if that were the dumbest idea he'd ever heard, and Mother's hands fluttered up, shooing away their doubts. "No, no, no, there's more than enough room," she insisted.

I couldn't help noticing what a thoroughly stunning romance-novel couple Fleur and Richard made. She was compact and petite, the top of her head barely reaching his shoulder. He was a few inches taller than I was, if that. I felt like a giant praying mantis in fruit boots—boots with treads the size of truck tires.

Mother was asking them if they were hungry, but they said they'd had dinner on the road a couple of hours before. "How about something hot to drink then?"

"Russian tea, I hope," Bjorn said.

Mother nodded and turned to go back into the kitchen. "Kate, I need your help for a few minutes," she said to me.

Dad offered to help with the luggage, and they all moved toward the front door. I wanted to follow them out to the driveway and be inches away from Richard Bradshaw, whom I hadn't seen in four years, and see if he ever looked my way, if he was feeling anything like I was feeling, but my mother had saved me from myself.

"Bjorn hasn't changed a bit," she said when I entered the kitchen. "He's still a pied piper, bringing all of California home for Christmas without warning." She opened the refrigerator. "Throw this in the can, will you?" She handed me a brown chunk of lettuce. "You should have seen him; he ran all through the house first thing." Her head disappeared back into the fridge. "I don't think there are sheets on the bed in the guest room—just the spread."

"I'll check," I said.

"I'm going to put Trish and Bjorn in his old room, of course," she said, pulling out lemons and oranges. "Richard can sleep in the guest room." She handed me the fruit. "Do you suppose he and that girl want to share a room? He called her his friend. Is that a euphemism? Of course, if they really are just friends, then—"

I shrugged. "Beats me. Her name is Fleur, by the way." I began halving the fruit with a knife.

"Well, let's have Fleur"—her lips curved up slightly—"sleep in your room in the extra bed. Do you mind?"

No, I didn't mind. Better with me than with Richard.

"If the two of them want to get together, they'll more than likely find each other. Don't you think?"

I cut myself. "Makes sense," I said, sucking blood from my thumb. I hated this whole topic.

Mother handed me a paper towel. "Where is Miss Manners when one needs her?" she asked, pulling the sugar container out of the cupboard above my head. "Fleur St. Geranium doesn't seem like Richard's type somehow."

I snorted. "St. *Germaine*, Mother. She's pretty stunning, don't you think?"

She poured a cup of sugar into a boiling pot of water on the stove. "In a Californicated kind of way." She's shrewd, my mother is.

I smiled and whispered, "I don't think she's California bred. She drops her postvocalic 'r's' ever so slightly."

Mother looked skeptical.

"No, really," I said. "I think she's from the upper South or maybe the lower south Midland—Charleston, Baltimore maybe."

Mother wiped a spill on the stove. "You sound more and more like your father."

"Thank you."

"But"—she held my shoulder—"I hate to tell you this, Ms. Linguist, but she was raised in Newport Beach, California. We established all that before you arrived."

I checked her face to see if she was serious. Irony is a family trait. "You're kidding," I said. "That doesn't seem right," and I left to check the bedding.

Mother was right about the bed in the guest room; it had no sheets on it. I chose pale blue ones with striped pillowcases for Richard. Then I made space in my closet for some of Fleur's things and checked out the bathroom, which was in pretty decent shape. All I really had to do was put out extra towels. I could hear Bjorn and Richard moving up and down the hallway with suitcases, reminiscing together like two old men. "Hey, this is

19

the closet where we lost your gerbil, Werner von Braun
—remember?" Richard asked.

"Probably still in there," Bjorn said.

"Probably the size of a cocker spaniel."

Their voices floated into the bathroom, where I looked into the mirror to determine how I'd changed since I was thirteen, when Richard had seen me last. My hair was much shorter, for one thing, and my braces were gone. The glasses remained of necessity. Was I pretty? It's hard to make judgments about your own face. My dad says I'm intelligent and that's the important thing. Mother says I'm wholesome-looking. Give me a break. Standing there in the bathroom, hearing Richard's voice, his "full and masculine laugh"—I copied that from the phrase book, but it's true—I was willing to drop twenty-five IQ points in exchange for looking exactly like Fleur St. Germaine.

LATER WE SIPPED Russian tea, made with cinnamon sticks borrowed from the neighbors, from Santa Claus mugs in front of a blazing fire in the living room. The first thing Bjorn saw was the Christmas tree, my mother's tiny, perfect work of art, placed carefully on the grand piano. "That's it?" His voice rose like a boy's. "That's the tree?" He stood next to it. "It's pathetic."

"Feel free to speak your mind, Bjorn dear. Don't be shy," Mother said.

Trish, who sat next to Mother on the sofa, said, "Mind your own business, Bjorn!"

Bjorn feigned a churlish look. "Excuse me, but this *is*

20

my business. Tell me if I'm wrong, but didn't we always have a huge tree with all these wonderful ornaments on it? Wasn't that the *tradition* in the Bjorkman household?"

"You mean wonderful ornaments like that little sled made of Popsicle sticks that you made in Cub Scouts?" Mother's arched eyebrows created pleasant lines in her forehead.

Trish, smirking, nudged her.

"No," Richard said, "he means the boondoggle candy cane. I know that was *my* mother's favorite." He grinned at Mother.

"Yes, that was a very good year, the boondoggle year," Mother agreed.

"Actually, my favorite was the pinecone Santa Claus that we made in fifth grade with Mrs. Seely. Remember?" Bjorn was asking Richard. "We used red and white felt."

"And a gallon of that white glue. But it was supposed to be an elf," Richard said.

"No, it wasn't."

"Yes, it was."

"You guys, nobody cares," Trish said.

"We made pinecone *mice* when I was in third grade." Fleur startled me when she spoke. We had been sitting in the window seat together and I had somehow—through osmosis, I guess—gotten the idea that she was shy and that we would have to ask her questions to draw her out.

"Mice" was the operative word here. Bjorn and Richard simultaneously clamped their hands over their mouths. "Don't ever say the M-word in front of Boo!" Richard said.

"Singular or plural M-words make her very nervous," Bjorn said.

Fleur turned her dazzling head my way. "The M-word?"

"You guys!" I yelled. They were always going to keep me frozen at age thirteen. It was hopeless.

"M-I-C-E." Richard spelled it slowly. "Or M-O-U-S-E. Never"—he squinted for emphasis—"say those in Boo's presence."

"You guys are such dorks. Don't give them any satisfaction, Fleur," I said. "Don't ask a single question."

- Trish held up her hands for quiet. "Better let Tweedledee and Tweedledum just tell the story. Maybe they'll wear themselves out." She smiled in my direction. "Tell it, but tell it fast," she directed.

"It was in early spring," Richard began.

"Late winter," Bjorn corrected. "We were having one of those unusual early thaws."

"Which one is Tweedledum? That's what I want to know," Fleur said.

"I'm Dee; he's Dum," Bjorn said.

"A judgment," Richard said, "from a man who doesn't even know the difference between Santa Claus and an elf." The fingers of both hands circled the mug as if to keep his hands warm. Very nice hands. "I was there first," he said, continuing the story. "I heard her screaming her head off out in back."

"It was early spring," I said.

"And?" Fleur prodded.

"We were all at Midgely's house," Richard continued.

"He was the tennis coach at the high school, but he also taught everybody in this neighborhood how to play—"

"He lives across the street," I said. I decided not to mention the cancer.

"Anyway, Katie—she wasn't Boo yet then"—Richard grinned at me, and I felt a "warm glow" flow through me, as the phrase book says—"Katie was there with that ditzy friend of hers—"

"Ashley," I said.

"Ashley Cooper," Bjorn said. "She always had the hots for you, Rich."

Richard winced. "And Boo, I mean Katie, asks Midgely if she can use the Lobster to practice her backhand."

"The automatic tennis machine?" Fleur asked.

Richard nodded. "Midgely tells her it hasn't been used all winter and that she'll have to take it out of the shed and roll it onto the tennis court. So she goes out alone—"

Bjorn couldn't stand to have Richard telling the entire story by himself, and he picked it up: "She's gone about ten minutes when we hear this tremendous screaming from the tennis courts—just bloody awful screaming. And Rich runs out to see what's happening."

Richard continued: "There's Katie, screaming her head off, as these baby mice come shooting out of the Lobster at regular intervals. There must have been a nest of them there for the winter. Some came flying over the net and landed at her feet. Some even survived to scurry around. A few landed in the net, and one actually stuck

23

to her tennis racket and she tried to shake it loose, screaming her head off at the same time."

"And he just stood there and laughed at me," I said.

"I couldn't help it." He "smiled broadly" at me. "You looked so funny with those mice scurrying around your feet." He liked the memory, I could tell. "But what was so great was when everybody was out there laughing, she got mad at us and started whopping the mice with her racket as if they were balls and she was playing tournament tennis." Was it my romantic imagination or was there an edge of tenderness in Richard's voice when he said this? I remembered he had yelled, "Go for it!" when I began swinging at the mice.

"I don't think anybody ever did think to turn off the machine," I said.

"You hit innocent mice?" Fleur asked.

"It was self-defense," I said.

"We were enjoying it too much to turn it off," Richard said. "That's when we started calling her Boo," he said.

Fleur gripped my knee. "You should have hit *him* over the head with your racket," she said, nodding at Richard.

I laughed. "Would you have done that?" I asked.

"I would have hit him with my car," she said.

I didn't have the heart at the end of chapter two to reveal to you what I'm going to reveal now in Chapter Three, and that is that when Fleur said she would have hit Richard with her car, instead of "locking eyes" with Richard, as the phrase book says, I locked eyes with Fleur. With a girl! It's true. We shared a "knowing look." In the background I was aware that Richard said to her, "You'd run me down with a steamroller," but it was as if he were speaking from the far end of a tunnel, because my attention was on Fleur's power.

"I could learn something from you," I said.

She extended her hand and we shook. She had a firm, confident grasp.

Bjorn said, "Now that's all we need is Fleur teaching Boo." I wondered what he meant.

I'll tell you another thing that's wrong with this novel besides the fact that the protagonist/antagonist relationship has gone seriously awry—I mean, I could tell the first night she was there that I wasn't going to hate Fleur at all, and if she was Richard's girlfriend, well, then, he was one hell of a lucky guy. Anyway, we decided, with Mother's blessings, to go out and buy a gigantic tree in the morning so that Bjorn could relive Christmas past and hang all the old ornaments of his recently spent childhood. Then we all went to bed, but not to sleep.

Richard's room was separated from my room by a shared bathroom. I felt inhibited by this. Even though I had to go pretty badly, I didn't want to, because, you know, maybe Richard had to go badly too, and I'd meet him in there and he'd say, "No, you first," and I'd say, "No, you first," but I'd have to go first, and I can't go under pressure. Sometimes, when I go to hear the St. Paul Chamber Orchestra, I have to go to the bathroom at intermission and I have to wait in line because it's winter and cold, which means everyone in the place has to go too, but then when I finally get into the stall, I just sit there, stunned, like a moose that's just walked into a tree. And I'm sure the other women standing in line can see me just sitting there through the gap between the door and the wall of the stall; there's always a huge gap.

While I was obsessing about bathroom sharing, Fleur said, "My bladder is just bursting," and rushed in there and sure enough, Richard's door opened at the same time and they collided.

"I get it first," Fleur yelled, and shoved Richard hard.

He shoved her back and said, "No way, French flower," and laughed in her face.

But Fleur managed to slip past and under him, and sat on the toilet, declaring, "Squatters' rights!" Then it was her turn to laugh.

I was afraid Richard would unzip his pants, but he

left, closing the door, which Fleur locked from her side. Immediately he began pounding the door. "Fleur, are you finished yet?" he called to her. "Fleur, are you finished? Hurry up, will you?"

Well, if that happened to me, I wouldn't be able to pee for the rest of my life, but Fleur went right ahead even though the door to my room was still open. There weren't any pauses. When she was done, she called to me, "Kate, do you want to go before Rich breaks the door down?"

I said I had to get some laundry from the basement and ran down there where there is a solitary toilet in the corner behind the water heater. It's an old thing with brown mineral stains in it, and I've avoided it all my life, but right then I was feeling mighty grateful for this odd fixture. I took a clean flannel nightgown back with me. Were they in love, Fleur and Richard? Was this pushing and shoving each other just sexual tension? I didn't know, but I wanted some.

When I returned, Fleur had changed into a long T-shirt and had picked a book of recent American short stories from my bookcase. She passed my desk and stopped. "What's this?" she asked, examining the papers on my desk. " 'Preliminary thoughts on Desdemona,' " she read. It sounded strange to have her reading my stuff aloud.

"I have to write a research paper on *Othello*, and I was thinking of doing it on Desdemona," I said. I pulled my arms through the sleeves of my flannel nightgown.

Her index finger followed through a list I'd made. "I

27

wrote about Desdemona for an advanced Shakespeare class," she muttered.

She was probably an expert. She read more of my notes aloud: " 'I hate it that Othello kills her when she's so innocent.' "

I began to wish I hadn't left the notes on my desk. "Lots of kids are writing about her innocence," I said. "I'd like to do something different, but I don't know quite what. I want a different approach." I pulled back the covers on the bed. "I'll think of something eventually. I always do." I sat on the bed.

Fleur turned, leaning back on the desk. "Her innocence has nothing to do with anything," she said. Her arms were folded loosely on her chest, teacher style. "I mean," she continued, "what if she *hadn't* been innocent? What if she'd slept with Cassio and Brabantio and the entire Italian navy?"

"Yeah?" My mouth probably hung open. I wasn't sure where she was heading.

"Would it be okay for him to kill her if she'd been sleeping around? What if he'd been right about her?"

"But he wasn't right—"

"But what if he were? What if she were guilty? Is it okay for a husband to kill his wife for adultery?"

"I've never thought about it," I said. "But no, it wouldn't be right, and yet we're all reading the play as if it's perfectly all right to—"

"Yes, we are!" She bestowed a full, benevolent smile on me. "Welcome to feminist criticism," she said.

Her smile melted me down like ice statues in a spring

thaw. I couldn't and wouldn't compete with her in a million years.

"If you want, I'll write the names of some articles down for you in the morning. Yours will be the only paper of its kind."

"I'd like that." I was lying on my bed, propped up on one elbow, my back to the window.

Fleur crouched over me to look out. "It's still snowing." She said it kind of breathlessly, as if snow were magic.

I turned to look. "We're going to have a perfect Christmas," I said. "It's supposed to snow for the next two days."

"A perfect Christmas." She seemed truly mesmerized by the falling snow. "That's why I came," she said softly.

"For the snow?"

"Yes." Then she seemed to change her mind. "Well, more than that, actually."

I wondered if she was expecting to get engaged at Christmas. I could not avoid the real possibility. I would have to let the *idea* of Richard and me go. It was an idea I realized I had built and nurtured in the last four years during his absence. It seemed entirely foolish at the moment.

Fleur sat lightly on the edge of my bed. "I've heard Bjorn and Rich talk about their families, and they, you know—" She seemed embarrassed, looking away from me and back to the snow. "Well, their families sounded so traditional and so—" She reached for the right word. "So wholesome." She glanced at me. "I wanted to spend

Christmas around people like that." Blushing made her even more beautiful, if that was possible.

"Your family are perverts?" I couldn't help asking.

She snorted. "No!" The blush instantly vanished. "But they're not the Brady Bunch either."

She shook her head. "They're not like your parents. Bjorn wasn't even exaggerating about them." She looked down at her hands.

I moved my legs to make more room for her on the bed. "So you like The Nels and Becca Bjorkman Show?"

She laughed. "And their perfect children, Bjorn and Kate Bjorkman."

"Bjorn's not perfect!" I grinned at the implication.

Fleur smiled and sat down on her own bed. "I'm going to read for a few minutes." She held up the book. "Unless the light bothers you?"

"No, it's fine," I said. "Really."

She snapped on the reading lamp by her bed and turned off the overhead light.

I took off my glasses to wipe my eyes. The room became an amorphous haze.

"Why don't you wear contacts?" Fleur asked from the corner. "You look really nice without glasses." She stopped. "I mean—"

"It's okay—I know," I said. "My eyes haven't been able to tolerate contact lenses so far, or I would have changed over years ago."

"How well can you see without them?" she wanted to know.

I laughed. "I know you're the shadow in the corner,

but if I didn't know this room so well, I wouldn't even recognize you as a human form."

"That bad, huh?"

"That bad."

"Mmm" was all she said.

"I'm used to it," I said. I put them back on.

Romance readers of America would probably want me to assess my feelings now. I'm well into the third chapter, after all, probably near the end, a good place to assess. The phrase book offers myriad feelings to choose from:

—*the pain in her breast became a sick and fiery gnawing?*

No, that doesn't sound like me at all. Although it was sad to know that I had built a fantasy around Richard—I thought I would grow up and he would see the light and marry me—if he got engaged to Fleur, I would have to give it up. And maybe even sadder was the realization that even if he didn't get engaged to Fleur, it might be time to give the fantasy up anyway.

—*her breasts rose and fell under her labored breathing?*

I was pretty tired, if you want to know the truth. My breathing wasn't at all labored.

—*mixed feelings surged through her breast?*

What is all this obsessive *breast* imagery? I hardly think of breasts ever, and here they are just bursting out at me from every page of the phrase book. Breasts everywhere: heaving and gnawing and lifting and pointing and panting. It's disgusting!

Across the street, Midgely's house was dark, except for one second-story window. Midgely was the one who had made them turn off the tennis machine years before, and had put his arm around my shoulder, asking, "You okay?"

And I had been, of course, especially when Richard had taken my racket and removed the squashed mouse from the strings and thrown it into a bush. "You're better off playing with balls," he'd said and had smiled at me in a way that made me feel like an equal and not just Bjorn's little sister.

Of course, then Bjorn had yelled, "Might say the same for you, Bradshaw," and there was a lot of snorting and chasing around, and the moment was gone. Still, I continually go back to that smile of Richard's after he pulled the mouse out of my racket.

And I go back to Midgely, who taught all of us to play tennis and insisted that we were all champions.

It hit me that the thousands of lights that usually decorated the trees surrounding Midgely's house at Christmas were missing this year. The house was the darkest on the block.

I removed my glasses, lay back, and sighed for Christmas past and Christmas present. I wanted Midgely happy at Christmastime.

Finally, I thought about Fleur preferring to spend Christmas with strangers.

None of it made any sense.

Revision Notes

I have just read what I've written so far, and already I can think of a thousand revisions I might want to make. I've left important things out. Should I go back now? What if I think of other revisions as I'm putting in the revisions? I'll never make it past chapter three! I think I'll just note my ideas down on this old stationery of Mother's in a different font and integrate them into the text later, as writers say. Here's a list of possible revisions:

1. Chapter one. My name. Even though my name (Kate) ends in an unvoiced dental plosive, that doesn't mean it's an unromantic name, as I imply in the prologue. Kate is, in fact, quite a romantic name. It is the female protagonist's name in Shakespeare's *Taming of the Shrew*, which is a romantic comedy. And there's a musical comedy called *Kiss Me Kate*. And Katharine Hepburn goes by Kate and she's a romantic leading lady. And so on. And so on.

So if I'm pushing myself as an unlikely romantic heroine (too tall, too owly), then perhaps for the sake of artistic continuity (writers say stuff like that) I should change my name in the novel to something a little more awkward—Inge? Ingeborg? Isak? Ingrid? I'm thinking Scandinavian here, since our family is Scandinavian. Gee, I really like the name Kate and find it hard to think of myself as Ingeborg even for the sake of art. I'll have to think about this.

2. Form. In the prologue, I say I want this romance

novel to end with "They lived happily ever after." Get real, Bjorkman! That phrase comes from fairy tales, not romance novels. I'll have to find a replacement from the phrase book.

3. Ashley Cooper. Twice I call her my best friend. Is that really accurate? Isn't Shannon my best friend? We have the same interest in language and poetry. She wants to edit this book for me when I'm done. Am I trying to mislead the reader? On the other hand, if I tell the reader everything in the first few chapters, then why write a book at all?

4. Bjorn and Trish. Nobody's going to believe that they got married between his junior and senior year in college. Why didn't they just—you know—do it and wait on the marriage stuff? How am I going to explain Bjorn when he makes up his mind? Stubborn. Even Trish was reluctant, but my big brother is persuasive. My parents tried to talk them out of it. They wanted Bjorn to finish college first.

Poop. Is it my business to explain Bjorn? He does what he wants. I guess I show that in the way he insists on buying a huge tree when we have a perfectly elegant tree in place on top of the grand piano. I could make him older for this novel, but then Richard, as his best friend, would be seven or eight years older than me. Gross. Bjorn got married because he wanted to and that's the truth. I don't know how to change it.

Did I mention that Trish is two years older than Bjorn and works as a photographer's assistant in San Francisco? She wants to be a photographer like Annie Leibovitz someday. Did I say that she brought her Hasselblad with her? Did I say I

like her? I do like her. I musn't forget to show that in the book.

⚘ 5. My height. Maybe some people will find it too grotesque to have such a tall romantic heroine, but, hell, it's my story! Besides, there are worse things than being tall: scales, warts, baldness, an underbite, missing limbs, chronic nosebleeds, halitosis, loss of bladder control—they're all worse. I come from a long line of tall women. My mother's as tall as I am. So is my grandmother, and none of us has ever been ashamed of it. At least that's what my mother told me in sixth grade when I felt like a textbook case of anterior pituitary overactivity and thought the top of my skull would burst through the ceiling at any second (and I was only five feet, eight inches tall then). Mother made me stand tall, said it was okay to be tall. I said I felt like an Amazon. She said wasn't it a nice feeling. Slowly, I began to believe it was a nice feeling.

6. My mother. She sounds like a housewife when she actually runs a full-time interior design business. The trouble is she takes two weeks off at Christmas and New Year's, so in this book she's home all the time. Is this even important enough to include in the novel? Artistically speaking, who cares if she's a housewife or a designer? She does, I'm afraid. It has to do with her as a character. I'd better work it in.

7. Chapter two. It's in deep doo-doo. I'm supposed to keep track of everyone in any given scene, and I didn't do a very good job with my father in chapter two. He never said a word through that whole scene in the dining room. But what am I supposed to do? He *really* didn't speak another word the

rest of the evening. Art copies life, after all. My father is an observer, not a participator. I think he married my mother, who is quite a bit younger than he is, to do the participating for both of them. Still, I should have acknowledged him by showing his reactions to the conversation. I could have had him tilt his head to one side, the way Ruffy, our beagle (now dead as Rin Tin Tin), used to do. Dad reminds me of Ruffy a little that way. Or I could have had him stroking my mother's arm as he sometimes does, but he was sitting across the room from her in the occasional chair by the fireplace with his feet resting on the footstool. He was, if I'm being truthful, sleeping through the whole retelling about me and the mice. In fact, my dad can hardly sit down socially with a group of people without falling asleep. My mother tells everyone he suffers from narcolepsy, but I think this is just to protect him from others. What else can she say? *You people bore my husband, so he's zonked off?* No, I don't think so. But I've never seen him sleeping in his study in front of the computer, with Bach or Telemann playing on the CD. He did sleep through most of chapter two, though. I guess I'll have to fix it.

8.   Violence against baby mice. That bit about my hitting the baby mice with a tennis racket sounds pretty cruel when it's all printed out on paper. Somehow I have to let the reader know that I began hitting them to show Richard and Bjorn that I wasn't afraid. That's no excuse, of course. I *did* hit baby mice with my tennis racket. Whacked them senseless. If I write that, will the animal protection people come after me? Could I go to jail? I did it, but I don't have to tell the truth

necessarily. I mean, I could make up some other story—a less violent story. I'll have to think about it.

9.   Chapter three. Bedroom scene with Fleur. It's undeveloped still. We talked about other things besides Desdemona and my eyesight. I mean, I did ask her about how she met Richard and Bjorn (in a history of civilization class—first year).

Then too, I asked her if she missed living at home. ("Home?" She said it as if it were a foreign word or something. I don't think she even answered me.)

And sure, I asked her about Stanford and stuff about California, but really, I didn't hear any of the answers, because I was thinking all the time about the THINGS I COULDN'T ASK FLEUR ST. GERMAINE:

   a.   Are you and Richard lovers? (Geez, I sound like I'm writing bad subtitles for an Italian movie.)

   b.   Are you going to be lovers much longer? (duh!)

   c.   What is the chance that you might find someone else and that Richard will become *my* lover? (Sounds like a virgin's fantasy.)

   d.   If there is a slim chance to no chance at all of your changing lovers, is it possible that you might have some horrific congenital disease that could cause your early (and yes, very sad) demise?

   e.   Does psychosis leading to suicide run in your family?

   f.   Why is it so hard to hate you?

I'm completely embarrassed by these questions. Is it possible to make writing worse with revision?

10.   Should I include in chapter three that I pretended to be asleep to see if Fleur would sneak into Richard's room? The reason I didn't put it in is because whenever I pretend to be asleep, I do fall asleep. So I really didn't learn anything.

11.   Richard. Probably I should include more memories of him. Like that time just before he moved when he dropped his chewed gum into the waste can under the kitchen sink, and when he left, I retrieved it and chewed it another hour. It was like French kissing with him, I thought.

No, I don't think I'll put that in.

Then there was that time up at Gooseberry Falls near Lake Superior when Richard and Bjorn climbed under the falls and Richard slipped and sliced his chin open. Blood gushed everywhere. He took off his T-shirt and held it wadded tightly against the wound as we hiked back to the road. Bjorn drove him to the hospital in Duluth. When the emergency room doctor began stitching on his chin, Richard laid the bloody shirt down on the table.

"You want me to throw this out?" I asked him, picking up the shirt.

"Yeah, might as well. Thanks, Boo."

I nodded and left. I hid the shirt under the backseat of the car. I still have it hidden in the bottom of my wicker chest at the foot of my bed.

Geez, I can't write this kind of stuff. I've never told anyone about this. It makes me sound obsessive, like Ashley. I don't

know why I kept the shirt. It's not as if I ever look at it or anything. I never do, as a matter of fact. But I've never thrown it out either.

There's that time when Richard and Bjorn were making out with these two girls in our living room after the senior prom. Richard was with Madelaine Dusendorf—that was her real name; I'm not changing the names of the guilty. I had gone down in what seemed like the middle of the night and got more than I bargained for. Richard and Madelaine were all enmeshed. Somebody was making wet, sucking noises. Really gross. His tie was nowhere to be seen.

I'm getting sick and depressed as I write this stuff down. It reminds me of something else. Something I don't want to think about. I don't want to think about any of this right now. I don't care about the silly revisions. Poop on the revisions.

"I'm not sure you're going to be able to find a tree two days before Christmas," Mother said at breakfast the next morning. This is Chapter Four, by the way. It was ten o'clock, and this was my second breakfast. My dad, who makes breakfast between semesters and on weekends, had busted himself with omelettes and hash browns and raspberry compote and freshly ground coffee.

"There's a place on Grand Avenue, I remember," Bjorn said. "Their trees were always overpriced and slow-moving. We'll try there first."

"Does everyone eat this well in Minnesota?" Fleur asked, and I could see my father's head tilt the way Ruffy's used to do, to the side, as if he'd heard his name. I knew he was trying to place a certain sound in her voice, maybe the slightly constricted mid-Central vowels, a sound that didn't come from Newport Beach, where she'd been raised. I could hear it too.

"Only on weekends," my mother said. "When *he* cooks. The rest of the time it's oatmeal."

"I'm glad I got here on a weekend." Fleur bestowed a full smile on my father, which did not go unnoticed. His ears grew pink. My mother noticed it too and laughed out loud, which made his ears grow even pinker.

"I love oatmeal," Richard said, explicitly for my mother. "Especially with apples in it."

She nodded at him. "With apples it will be," she said.

"What a brown noser," Bjorn said. "He always did kiss up to older women."

"You're just jealous," Trish said.

Bjorn bit her playfully on the neck. "What have I got to be jealous about? I've got you." He nuzzled her and she squirmed, delighted.

"Are we talking about older women like *me?*" Mother asked.

"He said it, not me," Richard said.

"It's all relative, my dear." My father kissed the back of Mother's neck.

I wondered if Richard would kiss Fleur's neck and make this happy sexual play at breakfast complete. To my relief, he seemed content to eat his omelette. Fleur watched my parents carefully.

The back of *my* neck itched considerably. I was happy when the back-door bell rang and I could get up to answer it.

Enter Ashley Cooper.

"I *knew* you were home, even though the answering machine said you weren't." She stepped into the back hall. "It dropped to eighteen below last night. The heat wave is over." She loosened her muffler and unzipped her parka.

"So what? You've got your love to keep you warm," I said.

She smirked. "Mmm, yes I do." She heard the commotion in the kitchen. "Are you guys still eating?" She looked down at her watch.

"Yes, come in. You'll never guess who's here—"

"Hi, Ash," Bjorn called.

Richard stood. "Hi, Ashley." He held out his hand.

Ashley clutched it in both of her hands. "My gosh," she gushed, not letting go of his hand, "I haven't seen you guys in ages. How are you?"

"We're brilliant, thank you," Bjorn said.

Trish punched him.

"I don't think you've met Trish." Bjorn was laughing.

"Oh, you guys got married in Hawaii last summer. I was so jealous when Kate got to go to Maui."

"Well, you went to Mexico—"

"Yeah, but Mexico—" She pretended to gag. "Driving through Mexico is nothing but dead animals on the side of the road."

"This is Fleur St. Germaine," Richard said. He had recovered his hand.

I could tell that Fleur stunned Ashley a little. There was a quarter note of a flinch when Ashley saw her sitting next to Richard. Not that Ashley skipped much of a beat. She doesn't give up her power easily. "How fun for you to be able to come," she said and actually patted Fleur on the shoulder. She was smiling her barracuda smile. All the sharp little teeth showing. Her patronizing manner is the reason most girls hate her.

Fleur, who did not smile, said, "How fun for you to be able to meet me."

I think my father snorted over the frying pan, and Richard shook his head as he sat back down. Trish and Bjorn exchanged a look I couldn't read. You notice these things when you wear glasses the size of Dayton's Department Store.

"Sit down here, Ashley," my mother said, giving up her chair on Richard's other side.

"Oh, I couldn't," she said, sitting down in one clean motion. "Kate," she said, leaning across Richard, "do you want to go down to the Nicollet Mall this morning and do some last-minute shopping? I still have to find something for Kirk."

"Well, I guess . . ." I hesitated. I really wanted to go buy a tree with the others, but it suddenly occurred to me that maybe I wasn't invited. Maybe they still thought of me as a tagalong. Still age twelve going on thirteen. "I don't know why not—"

"No, you have to help us buy a tree!" Bjorn said. "It's your familial duty." He turned to Ashley. "She's going with us this morning."

I relaxed. I was invited.

I could see Ashley's brain cells regrouping. "I thought you had a tree already," she said. "The one on the piano—"

Bjorn waved his arm, erasing the very idea of such an insignificant tree. "I mean a *big* tree. A touch-the-ceiling tree. An old-fashioned Christmas tree."

"A macho tree," Trish continued. "An Arnold

43

Schwarzenegger tree. A tree with a trunk the circumference of a barrel."

Fleur picked it up: "A tree big enough for an eagle's nest."

"For a tree house," I said.

"A tree to hang yourself on," Mother drawled. She set a cup of coffee in front of Ashley and pushed the sugar bowl and cream pitcher gently in her direction.

"You guys are so crazy!" Ashley said and leaned into Richard, the way I had seen her do with dozens of boys in the last several years. It always seemed to work—that leading out with those tidy little boobs. The phrase book would describe those boobs as "firm high-perched breasts."

"That sounds so fun," Ashley was saying. "We never buy trees anymore. We have three synthetic trees—they reach to the ceiling, but they don't have that wonderful piney smell, even when Mother sprays them with a pine aerosol. It just doesn't work."

Fleur covered her eyes with a cupped hand.

"Well, why don't you go with them," Mother said. "It won't take that long, and you and Kate can go shopping later."

"Would it be all right?" Ashley was asking Richard, not anyone else.

Richard burped loudly, and I thought Fleur was going to lose it. "Perfect," she whispered under her breath.

" 'Scuse me," Richard said, his fist pressed against his smiling lips. "I seem to have lost control here." He let out a funny giggle, hiccuped, and started laughing helplessly.

"Just don't lose control of your sphincters," Bjorn said, pushing his chair back. "Or you go to a motel."

"Bjorn!" Mother said, but she was laughing.

Dad pulled a box of chocolates from the cupboard above the fridge and offered Fleur the first choice. "Dessert," he said.

Fleur blinked at the chocolates. "Professor Bjorkman," she said, "will you marry me?" She plucked out a dark cherry liqueur. "They're my favorites."

You should have seen my father blush. "Here," he said. "Take the whole box," and he handed it to her, laughing. No sign of narcolepsy this morning. No sirree.

This book could become dangerous. My father, age fifty-four, could fall hopelessly in carnal love with Fleur St. Germaine, leave my mother, age forty-five, and me, his computer, his classroom, his phonetic alphabets, and Minnesota, and go off to some beach somewhere with a twenty-one-year-old college student. It happens all the time. It happened to Ashley's mother and Ashley about eight years ago.

But this is not that kind of book. And my father is not that kind of man. He and my mother shared one of those damned "knowing smiles" that romance novels are filled with. He was just enjoying Fleur's beauty and her attention. She made him feel young. Maybe she even made him feel sexy. My parents fell in love twenty-five years ago. And they'll stay in love until they die. I'm the novelist and I know.

Richard was looking at Fleur as if he'd like a proposal of marriage himself, or was that my paranoia? Fleur had passed the box of chocolates to him, and he offered the box to Ashley without taking one himself. She took one wrapped in gold tinsel, unwrapped it slowly, and said to Richard, her lips about an inch and a half away from his, "This is a *special* one," and then fed it to him.

He didn't exactly pull away. It wasn't as if I could blame her or anything. Ashley was doing what she'd been doing with any guy in reach since I had known her. I remember the time she told me about "the lure." She made it sound like fishing, and she herself was the bait. We were in my bedroom in front of the dresser mirror. "Puff your lips out a little like this—no, part the lips slightly—yes, good, and move your chin forward, half closing the eyes. Oh, it doesn't work with you! Your glasses absorb your whole face."

It was true; I wasn't right for vampy looks. "Can't you just get a boyfriend by having common interests?" I asked her.

"Who do you know who enjoys identifying esoteric American dialects and keeping a journal written in the phonetic alphabet?" she asked me. She was practicing the pout in the mirror.

"My father."

"Gross."

"I wouldn't mind finding someone like my father. I like my father."

"He's always sleeping."

"No he's not. He's intelligent. He's funny. He's kind and sensitive. He loves classical music—"

"Borrring!"

"And he's a terrific dancer." I realized that my father

46

fit the descriptions found in the personal ads in the back of his college alumni magazine.

"None of that counts," Ashley said, finally turning away from the mirror to look at me.

"What counts?"

Her tongue flickered between her teeth. "Thighs," she said slowly. "Boys' thighs."

That was it? Thighs? *Thighs?* What about warmth and kindness and humor? What about intelligence and stability? But then I remembered that Ashley's father hadn't had a lot of those qualities and bit my tongue.

Richard Bradshaw is the only boy I've ever known who has the above-listed qualities. He wasn't in a whole lot of pain when she fed him a second chocolate.

On the other hand, I was miserable. Ashley could get anyone she wanted anytime she wanted. She leads out with her breasts, after all. And she's so sexy. I can see that she is. I have never competed with her for a guy. I know I could never win. And perhaps that's why we have been able to be friends. I have always been a willing listener to Ashley's escapades.

It was too painful watching Richard eating, literally, out of her hand. I would not be able to listen to her talk about him, ever. I could feel my shoulders slumping along with my morale. It took all my strength to keep my head from rolling forward and clunking onto the table.

Fleur probably had him all wrapped up, but if she didn't, Ashley would know what to do. Why did mating have to involve these stupid little games that I didn't know how to play? Didn't even want to play.

47

Then it hit me. Ashley didn't know how I was feeling. She was always telling me about her feelings, which were varied and extreme, and I tried to be sympathetic, although once she accused me of not understanding passion. Well, I understood it now. I would have to tell her. She would understand if anyone would. Honesty would work. I would be honest with her: *Look, Ashley, Richard is the only hero I'm interested in. I need your help in getting him. You could tell me how. Tell me how to puff out my lips. Tell me the magic words, Ashley. You're my best friend. Teach me. Remember how I helped you through algebra and through first-year German? I have been a good friend, haven't I? Now you have to be my friend and teach me how to get Richard. He's the only passion I've ever had. Besides linguistics.*

"Do you have time to go with us?" I asked Ashley, coming out of my reverie.

She looked away from Richard, startled, as if she'd forgotten that there were other people in the room. "Yes, I'd love to go—that is if there's room."

"You can sit on Richard's lap if there's not," said Fleur, standing up and gathering every dirty dish within reach. She looked mad.

"Take the Cherokee," Dad said. "That should hold all of you."

"I've got to brush my teeth," I said. "Ash, come upstairs with me, I've got something to show you."

Reluctantly she pried herself loose from our hero's side.

"What is it?" she asked when we were alone in my bedroom. "Your mother didn't buy you diamond earrings for Christmas, did she?"

48

"Diamond earrings? I don't want—"

"If I don't get them, I will kill my mother." She sat on my bed. "I've told her I don't want one other thing, just diamond earrings."

"Ash, listen—"

"Is the Ice Queen sleeping with you?" Ashley had spotted Fleur's duffel bag next to the bed.

"Fleur? Yes."

"She wanted to kill me when she saw Rich liked me." She let out this hormonal squeal. "Isn't he beautiful, by the way? What a surprise to find him here."

"Yes—I mean, yes, he *is* beautiful. I think so too." I'd never in my life said anything so dumb out loud. "I—I mean," I continued, stammering, "I mean, I like Richard, that is, Rich."

"Like him?" Ashley said. *"I crave his body."*

I swallowed. "So do I," I said, sitting on the bed next to her. "So do I—crave his body, I mean."

She looked at me as if I had developed an unpleasant facial tic. *"You?"* And then burst out laughing, obviously because it was the funniest thing she'd ever heard.

"Yes, me. What's so funny?"

"Well," she managed to say between giggles, "you're just not his type at all. I mean—" She stopped when she saw my face, which I know was not smiling. "You're serious! I can't believe it; you're serious."

I had never talked about Richard to anyone. To speak aloud about him was to make him a schoolgirl's fantasy, even if I was a schoolgirl. It made us both seem silly, but especially me. I felt that now as I talked: "Yes, I'm serious, and I want your help. You're the only one who can help me. I don't know how to attract someone like him. I've had no practice, no interest before this, really, but now I'm interested." I shook her shoulders. "I'm interested. Help me *lure* him." I used her word and felt immediately embarrassed.

"But *I* want him," she said, her voice rising.

"You have Kirk. You have anyone you want. Please —Richard Bradshaw is the only guy I've ever found who remotely interests me. He is the love of my life!" I was using a language she would understand. I didn't like the way it sounded coming out of my mouth. Sappy romance language. Ugh.

"So this is the cool Kate Bjorkman in love." Something, the tone in her voice, made her sound a little jealous of that cool Kate Bjorkman. "Hell has frozen over at last," she continued. And then, hugging me effusively, "Of course I'll help you," she said. She clasped her hands in front of her as if she were beginning a painting. "Take off your glasses," she commanded. "And keep them off. He's not going to look twice at you with those Coke bottles on your face." She removed them for me.

Even as close as I was to her, her face blurred. "How will I see?"

"You want him, don't you?" she said. "Then you'll have to give up seeing for a while. You're not wearing lip gloss," she said. "Didn't I give you some?"

"Oh, I keep forgetting—"

"Let me fix your face a little." She pulled makeup out of her coat pockets. "I keep this stuff to freshen up during the day," she said.

50

She did something to my lashes and eyes and applied more lipstick and gloss and blush.

"He'll fall on his head when he sees you."

"I won't be able to see it," I said. If he looked at me with yearning, I wouldn't see that either.

"Come on," she said, and pulled my arm. I put my parka on and slipped my glasses into the pocket.

Ashley must have seen me do that because she said, "Don't wear them under any circumstances."

I followed her down the stairs. "Shouldn't he fall in love with me with my glasses on, since I can't live without them?"

"Trust me," she hissed back. "I know about these things."

The others were ready to go in the kitchen in Chapter Five.

"Where are your glasses?" asked my mother, my father, Bjorn, and even Richard simultaneously—everyone who had known me all my life with those glasses welded to my face.

"In my pocket," I said as casually as I could. "They were giving me a headache." It was stupid, but I couldn't think of anything else. I couldn't see without them. Everybody knew. I felt like a total jerk. Ashley must have sensed these feelings, because she pinched my arm, which meant I was to go through with this.

"You look different," my dad said. I didn't usually wear makeup.

"Let's go before all those trees are gone," Bjorn said, to my relief. We headed out through the back porch and into the garage.

"Doesn't she look different, though?" my dad was asking my mother.

The last thing I heard Mother say before the back door closed was "Shhh."

A surprise awaited me in the garage. Bjorn and Trish were in the bucket seats in the front; Fleur sat on the far side of the backseat, then Richard, and before I could get in and sit next to Richard, which seemed to me to be a good plan, Ashley climbed in next to him. "Lucky you," she said to me. "You get the back all to yourself."

I couldn't believe it. I walked around the Cherokee, tripping over a snow shovel that I couldn't see, opened the hatchback, and got in with the sandbags my father keeps there in case we get stuck on ice.

Bjorn revved the engine.

"Wait a minute," Fleur said, opening her door. "I'll go back with Kate."

"You don't have to," I said.

"I want to," she said, climbing through the hatchback and closing it.

To tell the truth, there wasn't a whole lot of room, but I was grateful for Fleur. Even without glasses I could see that Ashley sat closer to Richard than she needed to. Old habits must be hard to break, I thought.

Just barely out of the neighborhood, at the corner of Cleveland and Larpenteur, Richard said, "We used to get all our trees there." I knew he meant the Boy Scout lot on the corner.

"We did too," said Bjorn.

"Let's stop in," I said. "They always have a good variety to choose from."

I heard Ashley let out a snort.

Bjorn yelled from the front, "Right. We'll just do that," but the car didn't slow down any.

Richard turned in his seat, his voice close to my ear. "Boo, for heaven's sake put your glasses on. How can you stand not seeing anything?"

"The Scout lot is completely empty. They've evidently sold out," Fleur said, a smile in her voice.

I shrugged it off. "I wasn't looking."

"You weren't *seeing*," Bjorn shouted from the front.

"That too," I said.

"Have you got your glasses with you?" Trish asked.

Fleur was already digging into my pocket. She pulled the glasses out and set them on my face. "Let there be light," she said.

"Oh, don't," Ashley cried. "She looks so much better without them. Don't you think so, Rich? Don't you think Kate looks better without her glasses?"

Oh, Ashley, shut up.

"Is it relevant?" Richard asked. "She can't see without them."

"I know, but if she could see, don't you think she looks better without glasses, really now, don't you?"

Shut up, shut up, shut up.

He turned, and I could see the tiny creases around his eyes. "Boo isn't Boo without those glasses," he said, and with his index finger he pushed the nosepiece playfully back up on my face and grinned at me.

Thank you, Lord, I thought.

"Kate is Kate *with or without* the glasses." Fleur nudged his back. She refused to call me Boo. Another reason to like her.

"Yes ma'am, I stand corrected. Fleur wouldn't be Fleur without the corrections," he said, turning forward again.

Ashley laughed too loudly.

At Trish's suggestion, we sang "O Tannenbaum" in German all the way to Grand Avenue, with Ashley giggling and saying, "Oh, I've forgotten the words. It's been years since I took German!"

Like last semester, I thought.

It turned out that Bjorn was right about the tree lot on Grand. They still had trees. He parked the car, and Fleur and I untangled ourselves and climbed out the back. We had gotten in the car while it was still in the garage, but now the cold hit us like a wall. Fleur covered her nose with both hands. "My gosh," she said.

I laughed. "The hairs in your nose freeze right away when it gets this cold," I said. I pulled my parka hood up and tied it securely under my chin. Then I noticed that Fleur wasn't wearing a hat at all.

"Here, take my muffler and put it around your head. You'll never survive without something on your head."

She didn't argue, but gratefully accepted the muffler.

We followed Bjorn and Trish into the lot. Trish held on to his arm, taking little, bouncy, excited steps. "Just think," she squealed, "we're buying our very first tree."

Ashley, imitating Trish, put her arm through Richard's and said, "Just think, Rich, you and I are buying our very first tree together."

He looked down at her, surprised, I think, but laughed as if he liked the joke. He turned and glanced at Fleur, a wry look on his face. Depressing.

Fleur put her arm through mine. "Let's go steady," she said, matching Ashley's voice exactly.

"Let's get married," I said, patting her arm.

"Let's have a family," Fleur went on. "A girl for you, a girl for me." She fluttered her eyelashes. "Just think, we're buying our first tree together." We burst out laughing.

Richard had disengaged himself from Ashley and was pulling out the tallest trees he could find.

"How about this, you guys?"

Bjorn had pulled out another one almost identical to the one Richard was showing us, a spruce. It was the kind our family always bought. The branches on both trees were frozen up, but you could tell they would thaw into a nice, symmetrical design—perfect for showing off ornaments.

"Oh no, not one of those," Trish said. "They're so skinny. They look undernourished. This is perfect." She held on to a fat piñon pine—our family called them the porcupine trees.

"But honey," Bjorn said, "the ornaments just sort of hang on the outside of those trees. They're so thick you can't get anything between the branches."

"No, they look wonderful that way, really. Our family always had a tree like this. Honey, this is perfect."

"Well, how about this one?" Bjorn pulled out another tree that looked exactly like the first one he'd shown her. "It's a little thicker near the top."

"Honey, it isn't a piñon pine."

"Or this one." Bjorn pulled out yet another spruce from the pack.

"Well, honey, I like this one." Trish pulled out another piñon pine and tried to push the frozen branches down with her gloved hand.

"That's nice, honey, but I like this one better." Bjorn wasn't listening. "What do you think, Rich?"

"Either one is fine with me."

"Well, I like this one," Ashley said, pointing at the tree Richard had chosen. "I think it's perfect."

Fleur smirked.

"I think we should get this one," Bjorn said. He shook the tree vigorously.

Trish scanned the lot. She seemed nervous. "Honey, let's look just a little more. We just got here." She walked down the aisle of trees.

Fleur stomped her feet. "It's freezing," she said. "I've never been so cold."

Bjorn called to Trish, "Honey, Fleur is cold. Let's go. This one will be fine."

Fleur started, "No, I didn't mean—"

"I like this one," Trish called from the end of the aisle. Another piñon pine.

"It might be fun to have a different kind of tree this year," I said to Bjorn.

"I hate piñons. They look like overgrown bushes," he said under his breath.

"Honey, come and look," Trish called to him again.

Richard began pulling ridiculous-looking trees, with huge sections missing, trees two feet high, from the racks. "I want this one," he said. "No, this one. This one is my favorite." Ashley, Fleur, and I laughed harder than we needed to, but we all wanted to get away from Bjorn and Trish.

Bjorn walked down the aisle to where Trish held her choice. He took the spruce with him. They huddled together in a whispered conference.

"Here." Richard continued his antics. "This one can be used for a swordfight. Hold on to this," he said to Fleur, handing her the most emaciated-looking little tree on the lot. She took it from him. He chose another almost like it and they began fencing. Fleur used both hands to hold the tree and went after Richard like a terrier after a rat.

Ashley grabbed a tree and went for Richard's back.

"Hey, no fair," he cried. He grabbed one end of the tree Ashley was holding and swung it around. Fleur hit him from behind.

Down the aisle, Bjorn and Trish were gesturing at different trees. Bjorn was doing most of the talking; Trish looked more and more defeated. Once in a while I heard an isolated "but honey" from her. Soon Bjorn strode back down the aisle holding the spruce like a victory lance. "We decided on this one." *We?*

Trish smiled weakly, then looked down at her feet, then up over the fence, across the street, anywhere but at any of us. I felt sorry for her. Even though I did like the tree Bjorn had chosen better than any of the piñon pines, I also knew what it was like to be railroaded by Bjorn. He was pigheaded sometimes.

Richard, Fleur, and Ashley put their "swords" back and followed Bjorn to the shack at the far end of the lot. We all went inside. A guy with mossy teeth—the kind of teeth so greenish and repulsive that you can only stare at them—sat in a lawn chair just inside the door.

"How much?" Bjorn asked.

The man told him. The price startled Bjorn. His head jerked up involuntarily.

Richard saw it too. "I have some money with me," he offered.

"Piñon pines are cheaper," the man said.

"Well, if they're cheaper—" Trish started.

But Bjorn was already paying the man. "It's fine," he said.

"How about some ornaments?" The man nodded into the corner. "My wife and her friends make them," he said.

The ornaments, mostly crocheted stars, hung by strings from the low ceiling.

"Oh, let's get some. Aren't they beautiful?" Trish's energy level was back. "These are just wonderful. Bjorn?"

"Honey, I don't have any more money—really," he said.

"But honey, they're not that much."

"Honey, please—"

You'd have thought we were in a beehive with all that "honey" flowing about.

"Thanks a lot," Bjorn said to the man, and opened the door of the shack. A blast of cold air hit us.

Trish turned back for a last look at the crocheted stars.

Bjorn and Richard tied the tree to the top of the Cherokee and we were off for home. It was a very quiet ride back.

* * *

59

THE FRONT HALL looked like a Dutch flower garden when we got home. Mother had brought all the potted tulips up from the basement. They were wrapped in dark green shiny paper with red ribbons. "Where did you buy tulips at this time of year? They're absolutely lovely!" Fleur said.

Richard had picked up one of the pots. "She forces them herself. This neighborhood would be in crisis if Mrs. Bjorkman stopped giving away tulips at Christmastime."

"Hardly," Mother said, pulling her coat out of the closet. "Did you find a tree?"

"We got a great one. I'm going to let it thaw in the garage for a while, and we can decorate it tonight." Bjorn rubbed his hands together like sanding blocks. "It'll be great," he said. Trish, who had followed him into the hall, walked around him and went upstairs without a word to any of us.

Mother's eyes followed her briefly.

"I want to learn to force bulbs," Fleur was saying.

"Oh, it's simple," Ashley said, squeezing herself between Fleur and Richard. "Anyone can do it."

Mother pursed her lips. "True."

Bach's *Goldberg Variations* floated in from the study.

"Play Christmas music!" Bjorn shouted to Dad.

"What?" Dad shouted back.

Bjorn repeated himself.

"I can't hear you; I'm playing *The Goldberg Variations.*"

Bjorn shook his head and went into Dad's study. "Hey, old man," we heard him say before he shut the door.

"Are you making the deliveries now?" Richard asked Mother. "Mind if I come along?"

"I would love the company. Fleur, would you like to come too? I can show the two of you off to the neighbors."

She made them sound like a couple.

I turned to Ashley. "You want to run down to the mall now? This is as good a time as any."

She looked at her watch. "No, I told Mom I'd be back to help her with the rest of the Christmas baking." She looked at Richard when she said this.

"Really?" I said, stunned. Ashley never helped her mother with anything if she could avoid it.

"Yeah, see you." She turned to Mother and the others. "I guess I'll be seeing you again in a little while." She knew Mother always gave them a pot of tulips at Christmas, and she wanted to be there. Totally transparent.

I followed her to the back door. "What's up, Ash?" Might as well be direct.

"What do you mean?" She was retying her muffler, trying to avoid my eyes, but I willed her to look at me. It's a power I have.

"Well, okay," she said when she finally stopped fiddling with her muffler. "I have to be honest with you." She licked her lips nervously, pressed them together, ran her tongue along her upper lip—she was getting ready to lie. "Kate, really, I don't think you have a ghost of a chance of getting with Richard. I know it hurts to hear it—" Her voice got more efficient. "See, you've let your lip gloss wear off." She pulled some out of her pocket, uncapped it, and was moving to apply some to my lips.

I caught her wrist in midair. "I don't think lip gloss is the solution here."

"And that's what I'm saying. There's so much—" She caught herself.

"So much wrong with me?"

"No, it's not that!" She fumbled with the cap of the lip gloss, which dropped to the floor. "It's just that—" She stopped to retrieve the cap. "I—"

"You're in love with Rich yourself and you can't let go. It's too important to you." I tried to keep my voice flat.

She looked relieved and clasped both my shoulders. "You understand, don't you? He's different from anyone I've ever known. He's so much more mature, for one thing. He's just so *nice*. I just can't help myself!" She let out a shrill giggle.

"Yeah, I know—it's his thighs," I said.

"Oh, you *do* understand, don't you." She gave me a feigned kiss on the cheek and a half-hug. "You understand everything," she said, leaving me in her wake of freezing air.

I looked at myself in the mirror Mother had hung by the back door. The lip gloss had worn off, just as Ashley had said. It didn't matter. The overall effect of my face was that of a goldfish looking out of its bowl. Nice skin. Nice hair. Nice person. Smart too.

Mother was pulling brown paper grocery sacks out of a drawer in the kitchen while Fleur and Richard brought in the tulips.

"They'll need protection from this cold," Mother said.

I stood in the entranceway watching all of them. "You'll probably be invited to lunch at Ashley's," I said. They were placing individual pots of tulips in the sacks.

"What makes you think so?" Mother said.

"Because Ashley's in love with Rich's thighs."

I loved their reaction, heads popping up simultaneously. I walked past them and turned before entering the dining room. "She loves his"—I let my tongue rest between my teeth and said it slowly—"thighs."

I could hear Mother and Fleur laughing as I went upstairs. "No offense intended, Rich, but Ashley loves everyone's thighs," Mother said.

I was at the top of the stairs when Richard called to me from the hallway. "Hey, Bjorkman!"

I turned and looked down at him. His arms were filled with tulips.

"Yeah, Bradshaw?"

"What I want to know is, what do *you* think of my thighs?"

My face got all hot, but this was no time to get tongue-tied, so I leaned over the banister. "I like your thighs—yes—but I'm especially fond of your *buns*." I smiled my most expansive smile.

Our eyes locked for the first time. *The Romance Writer's Phrase Book* would say: His "eyes caught and held" mine. He "captured" my eyes with his. And I thought I "detected laughter in his eyes."

"Why don't you go with us?" he asked.

"I'd better do some shopping," I said. I didn't want to

see Ashley again today. "Besides, I'm plumb out of lip gloss."

He laughed. "That is a crisis! See you later."

"See you." Our eyes held a few seconds longer.

Maybe we could be friends, I thought. Friendship had a better prospect for longevity than romance, and I wanted Richard Bradshaw for life.

I knocked on Trish's door, but she didn't answer, or she was asleep.

I spent the rest of the afternoon shopping for our unexpected Christmas guests. I had sent gifts for Bjorn and Trish weeks ago with Mother's packages, but I wanted them to have something from me to open under the tree on Christmas morning. Trish was easy. I drove directly to Grand Avenue and bought her a dozen of the crocheted Christmas stars she had admired that morning, and then, remembering how much Bjorn liked the tree lights that looked like real candles, I bought him a couple of strings of those for their own tree—if they could ever decide on what kind they would have. Bjorn's pigheadedness had annoyed me, but the way Trish had withdrawn for the day irritated me as well. I searched around for Fleur and decided on an angora wool muffler that would look stunning on her. It cost more money than I could really afford, and I charged it on Mother's Visa, hoping she would forgive me and knowing I would be her slave for weeks to come.

I wandered through the mall for an hour and a half wondering what I could buy Richard but couldn't come up with the right thing. I wanted to buy him something special, but not too personal, and not so special that he would know I thought he was special, but special enough that he would be pleased.

Aaugh. The way I was thinking reminded me of Ashley, and that scared me more than anything. So I finally bought him a picture book of the Boundary Waters, where he and Bjorn had gone canoeing every summer. Not too special and not too clunky either.

Revision Notes

Why, I am asking myself, was I friends with Ashley Cooper for all those years? The reader will surely want to know as well. She used me in what seem to me now indefensible ways. In these last two chapters, I have made her selfish, calculating, and just plain hateful. The problem is I have described her accurately. The dialogue, too, is not imagined. It is exactly what she said.

I called to ask Shannon's advice. (If she didn't go to Key West every Christmas to visit her grandparents, she could have helped me through this mess last Christmas.) I asked her why she thought I had remained friends with Ashley.

"Easy," she said. "You're a caretaker."

This sounded like a label she'd picked up in a psychology class.

"What do you mean—caretaker?" And was that good or bad? I wondered.

"Well, you're nice. Too nice, maybe. You want her to feel good. You're willing to overlook a lot. And it's helped that the two of you have absolutely nothing in common—you never had to compete over anything or anybody." She paused. "Until last Christmas, that is. That's when you saw her for what she really is—B-I-T-C-H." When Shannon spelled, it meant her little brother was in the room.

Was that right? I tried to think.

"Are you working on your novel?" Shannon asked.

"Yes."

"Maybe you ought to tell about that third-grade birthday party of Ashley's—the one *without* the pony. You must have told me that story a dozen times when I first met you in middle school. It was your way of explaining why she had to eat lunch with us. I thought she was a case of strychnine myself."

"I don't know," I said.

"Write it and see how it feels." She was quoting Midgely.

So here goes nothing—the story of how Mr. Cooper left Ashley and Mrs. Cooper forever on Ashley's ninth birthday: he left without eating any cake and it was his favorite kind, caramel with whipped marshmallow frosting—the shiny kind.

I was there along with a half dozen other girls from Falcon Heights Elementary School, standing on the porch looking for prizes that had been hidden earlier among the flowerpots and wicker furniture. We were also waiting for Mr. Cooper to arrive with the pony that was to be the event of the party. "Everyone can have a turn riding it," Ashley had told us.

But Mr. Cooper arrived in his red Mustang convertible without the pony. He had Tom Cruise good looks: that same easy smile.

"Daddy, where's the pony?" Ashley's voice rose with an anxiety that made my own stomach knot up.

"Oh, Piglet, I forgot." He patted her head, his smile bewildered as if he hadn't heard of Planet Earth, let alone any pony. He seemed surprised to see us. "I've got to talk to

Mommy, Sweetums," he said, jumping the stairs two at a time.

From the porch we heard Mr. and Mrs. Cooper shouting in the kitchen at the back of the house. Ugly shouting with name-calling and blaming. I hunted furiously for the prizes on the porch and found a ball and jacks. "Oh, this is great!" I said to Ashley. *I can't hear your parents* was what I wanted to say.

"This is cool," Ivy Joy Miles said, turning a yo-yo in her fingers. She too looked at Ashley as if to say *I can't hear them. Honest.*

Ashley, a half-smile creasing her lips, was twitching behind her skin. "I chose the prizes myself," she said.

Her father left in ten minutes. Ten minutes that seemed like three hours. He called Mrs. Cooper "one glorious bitch." It is seared into my memory. Then he left. "See ya, kitten," he said, his voice completely altered from the loud cursing of seconds before. "See ya, girls." He even waved.

"What about the cake? It's your favorite!" Ashley called to him.

"Later, Piglet." He was already in his car, revving it. He spun out, spitting pebbles onto the sidewalk. Happy Birthday, Ashley.

THIS WRITING BUSINESS can be depressing. I don't want to think about Ashley and her motives for doing what she does. I don't really want her to be a rounded character. I don't want to think about her pathetic ninth-birthday party and the

pain behind her eyes when her father left for good. I don't want to take care of that pain any longer by being her friend. I don't want readers taking pity on her for one second. I want to damn her to hell. Maybe I could have her murdered—in the novel, at least. It would be a wonderful catharsis for me to have her run over by a semi. I could write it in great detail. Spend paragraphs on it. She'd be flattened roadkill, her blood oozing into the street.

I thought I was finished emotionally with Ashley, but she's come back like vomit. I can't write another word.

When I returned home from shopping in Chapter Six, Fleur and Richard, both wearing aprons, were fixing dinner. "Your parents went to a party tonight, so we're baby-sitting you," Richard said. "Think of us as your parents now." He threw some scallions into the food chopper and turned it on.

"I get to be the father," Fleur yelled over the chopper.

"That goes without saying. We all know you've had a certain kind of envy all your life and recognize your needs—"

"You don't have to speak in euphemisms for me," I said. "I've read Freud." I placed my packages on the kitchen table and took off my parka.

"Our baby is precocious," Richard said. He set a tray of taco chips and bean dip on the table.

"She takes after her father," Fleur said, laughing. "*Moi!*"

"Ahh, but her beauty comes from me, her mother," Richard said.

Fleur turned and pretended to look me over carefully. "She has your thighs, all right." She laughed harder.

"My thighs are nothing compared to his thighs," I said. "His thighs are *gorgeous!*" They laughed at my imitation, but then I felt guilty. Sort of.

Bjorn appeared. "What's all the noise in here?" he said, affecting good humor.

"Nothing much," Richard said, "just general admiration for my thighs."

"Good grief."

"Is Trish okay?" Fleur asked. "Dinner will be ready in about twenty minutes—enchiladas."

"Oh sure." Bjorn shrugged. "She'll be down in a minute. You guys ready to trim the tree?" He didn't sound nearly as enthusiastic as he had that morning. "I guess we should wait for Mom and Dad, huh?"

"They won't be back until late," I said.

"I'm your mom now," Richard said.

Bjorn rolled his eyes.

"Your real mom said to trim the tree without them," Fleur said.

Bjorn nodded. "Okay then," he said. "I'll go see if Trish is coming down." He took a chip off the tray and left again.

Richard whistled softly. "Methinks there is trouble in paradise." He opened the oven door for Fleur, who lowered the dish of enchiladas into the oven.

"There's always trouble in paradise," she said.

* * *

71

TRISH AND BJORN both chattered through dinner, but not with each other. Their eyes never met. Their conversation was constrained, fake. It was exhausting.

Trimming the tree was even worse. It visibly depressed Trish to be around Bjorn's chosen spruce. Mostly she watched the rest of us from the window seat, turning occasionally to gaze at the falling snow, a half-sullen expression on her face. To make up for Trish, Bjorn grew hyper. He talked nonstop: "You know when we were little, I had this Matchbox city built up under the tree—remember that . . . Rich? And Boo would come around and want to stick those little cars in the tree. She thought they were ornaments. It'd make us so mad. We'd get all the little cars lined up just the way we wanted them, and she'd come along, and, bingo, suddenly all the cars were in the tree again!" Abnormally loud laughter from him. We all smiled and nodded, except for Trish, who looked out at the snow.

"I never had Matchbox cars of my own," I said.

"Boo should have been a boy. She's tall and pretty athletic and she always liked boys' games . . ." Blather, blather, blather. I wished he would put a lid on it.

Fleur rolled her eyes.

The tree, which had to be trimmed at the top, reached the ceiling, and when it was decorated, it really was pretty spectacular-looking, or maybe it was just that it was the kind of tree Bjorn and I had grown up with. Bjorn certainly was pleased. "Isn't it great, honey?" he asked Trish, after turning on the tree lights and turning off the overhead lights. It was the first time he had addressed her directly all evening. He was hoping for forgiveness. I could tell. "Great, isn't it—hon?"

Trish turned her head slowly, her arms crossed in front of her as if she were cold. "It's perfect," she said flatly, and then she got up and left the room. The bedroom door closed upstairs.

So Bjorn decided it was time for Russian tea again and heated some up, ranting the whole time. If I'd had a stake, I would have thrust it through his heart and called it a mercy killing. Sure must be fun to be a newlywed at Christmastime.

We went to bed early. "I think I'd like to be thoroughly unconscious now," Fleur said. Amen and amen.

I awoke to voices. At first I thought it must be Mother and Dad coming home, but soon realized that it was Bjorn and Trish arguing. "Not so loud!" Bjorn was saying. "Do you want everyone in the house to hear you?"

"I don't care who hears me." Trish's voice rose hysterically. "The only time you ever listen to me is when I yell. You never listen! You never ask my opinion about anything."

I reached for my glasses, sat up, and peered across the room at Fleur. She was sleeping soundly. I wondered if she'd taken a sleeping pill.

"I will not be rational!" Trish's voice filled the house.

I searched for my robe at the end of the bed and stepped quietly into the hall.

"Look, I'm sorry, okay? I didn't know it was such a big deal." Bjorn's voice was lower, but not low enough. I didn't want to hear any of this. I wanted them to be like they were last summer on Maui: affectionate, humorous. I wanted them to be the prince and princess again: Trish with orchids in her hair, her bare shoulders glittering, Bjorn weighed down with leis around his neck. Was this just a few months later, this living happily ever after?

I crept down the stairs, remembering what Midgely had said last year in junior English: "Comedies end in marriage, but tragedies frequently begin with marriage." He was already sick then, already bald, already too thin. "But"—he had smirked good-naturedly at us—"it's the tragedy that makes life rich—" His voice had caught slightly. "Worth living."

The falling snow combined with the streetlamp outside lit the living room enough so that I could see a figure sitting in the window seat. I turned to go back, feeling too awkward to disturb him. "Boo?" he called.

"Oh, I'm sorry," I said. "I just wanted to get away from—"

"I know. Me too. Come over. It's quiet here."

I sat, my back against the window frame, facing him. He wore a white T-shirt, gray sweats, and white socks. No shoes. I suppose if I were following the phrase book's lead, I'd have to admit that I was aware of the "muscles rippling under his white shirt" and also admit that it "quickened" my pulse a little. I'd never been alone with Richard before. Never sat in the half-light of the window seat with him. It felt intimate. So intimate that I was afraid to speak and watched the snow instead. When I turned my head, he was watching me. I swallowed hard. "So," I said, "what's your tree of choice?" I suddenly knew how Bjorn felt. I needed to hear noise even if I had to make it myself.

He smiled. "Spruce, but I hope I'm open to other suggestions. You?"

"Well"—I thought for a second—"I'm quite partial to those aluminum trees with the fluorescent pink balls and pink lights—ones that spin slowly on a pedestal."

"I guess you'll decorate your living room to look like McDonald's."

"I'm very fond of orange vinyl seating, as a matter of fact—with matching oak veneer."

"Remind me not to marry *you*," he said.

"Don't marry me," I said.

"And don't have my children," he said.

"Don't have a rich and satisfying life with me," I said.

"Don't ever kiss me," he said.

"Never," I said.

"Shake on it." We held hands longer than was necessary to solidify our pact. Or maybe it was a pact of its own.

His gaze returned to the street. "I saw Midgely today. I wouldn't have recognized him."

I enjoyed his face in profile. "He isn't teaching this year, you know."

"Your mother told me, but I'm not surprised. I've never seen anyone look so sick—didn't even know anyone could *be* that sick and alive at the same time." His voice faltered. "Know what he said about you?" He turned.

"That I had the world's silliest backhand?"

"No. He said, and I quote: 'Kate Bjorkman is one of the true champions.' "

I laughed. "He says that about everyone." But I was pleased. "Besides, I'm not that good a tennis player."

He drew in his lips thoughtfully. "I don't think he was talking tennis."

"Mouse player?"

He laughed then. "Yes, that must be it. Kate Bjorkman is a true champion mouse player. That's what he meant."

"Midgely always makes me think of Dylan Thomas," I said. "I don't know if he did this with you guys, but he spent weeks on Thomas's poetry last year—and we were supposed to be studying *American* lit."

Richard nodded. " 'The Force That Through the Green Fuse—' "

" 'Drives the Flower,' " I finished with him.

"Did he make you memorize the whole thing?" Richard asked.

"All twenty-two lines."

"I miss him already."

"Mmm."

It had stopped snowing. It was piled three feet high on the lawn and even higher along the curb where the snowplows had pushed it out of the street. Halos glimmered around the streetlamp. My breath frosted the window when I leaned my forehead against it.

"Guess who else we visited?" Richard slapped the now famous thighs. "Dr. Bybee!"

"You're kidding. I didn't know Mother gave him tulips—"

"I don't think she does normally, but I was telling her

76

how unusual it must be to have a guy with a doctorate in music teaching in elementary school, and I was carrying on about learning to play the recorder in third grade—"

"I still have mine!" I couldn't help saying.

"And about the annual spring concert—we did a whole Gershwin program when I was in fifth grade." He grinned. "Anyway, your mother took me to see him and he made me play recorder duets with him. Not only that, he made your mother and Fleur play too."

I shrieked and then covered my mouth. "Mother and Fleur? Really?"

He laughed at the memory. "He had them playing 'Jingle Bells' within ten minutes."

I jumped up. "Come on, we have to play." I grabbed his arm and led him across the living room and into Dad's study, where I turned on the overhead light. We both squinted in the brightness. "They're over here." I pulled out the bottom drawer of Dad's credenza and pulled out two wooden soprano recorders—mine and Bjorn's. "Here," I said, handing Richard one. "There's music in here too." I pulled out "Easy Christmas Songs for the Recorder," along with an old folded-up music stand my mother had bought at a garage sale years ago, and set it up in front of the love seat, where Richard was already sitting. I sat next to him. "What do you want to start with?"

He smacked his lips and tried a scale and then grinned at me. "Just start at the beginning," he said.

"Okay," I said. " 'God Rest Ye Merry, Gentlemen.' " I turned and looked at him. "Ready?"

He nodded. His foot began to tap. "And one and two and three and four—"

We began. I felt a giggle rising in me and struggled to restrain it. We played most of three measures and then, caving into each other, broke into loud guffawing. We made these involuntary pig snarking noises in the backs of our throats, which made us laugh even harder. Snark, snark, gasp and snark.

That's how my parents found us: collapsed and howling.

"You kids been in the liquor cabinet?" Dad asked.

I shook my head. "We've been p-p-playing the r-r-r—these." I held up the recorder and continued snorting.

"You sound like Porky P-P-Pig," Richard snorted and got hysterical all over again.

Then Fleur appeared, wearing pajamas with feet in them.

"Did they wake you up?" Mother asked Fleur.

"As a matter of fact, no. Believe it or not, something louder is going on upstairs."

Remembering Bjorn and Trish's fight, Richard and I sobered up to some degree. We explained the situation to my parents.

"Oh dear," Mother said. "Well, we might as well stay down here until they're finished. Newlyweds should be left to themselves for the first fifteen years, don't you think, Nels?"

"I think they should be left alone for twenty-five years." My father slung his arm around Mother's shoulder.

"Don't you think you should go up? Talk to them or something?" I asked. "They might get a divorce over a stupid Christmas tree."

Mother, removing her overcoat, said, "It's hard to be newly wed."

"My experience with newlyweds is that they should be gassed," Fleur said.

Mother struggled to find the appropriate expression.

"Oh, I'm sorry!" Fleur's fingers covered her mouth when she saw Mother's sagging jaw. "I didn't mean Trish and Bjorn. My parents—that is, my mother is going to be newly wed for the sixth time on New Year's Day. One of her husbands once called her a silver-lined slut. My father's third marriage is breaking up even as we speak. His last wife broke his head open with a blender. I was thinking about them."

"Oh dear," Mother said again. "And poor Bjorn and Trish upstairs bludgeoning each other over a tree. We'd really better go up and knock on the door."

My father nodded. "Good night," he said, taking Mother's arm.

"Do you guys want to go back to bed?" I asked Fleur and Richard.

Fleur shook her head. "I'd rather give them a little time." She sat down in Dad's desk chair. "You guys play. I'll enjoy."

Richard and I, after a half dozen false starts, interrupted by fits of giggling, mostly mine, played peaceful songs of a town called Bethlehem, a baby called Jesus, and winged singers called angels. Silently I prayed for peace upstairs.

Revision Notes

I find I'm mad at Bjorn and Trish. Their marital problems are ruining my romance novel. I know there's supposed to be tension, but not theirs! I feel like taking them out. But then why would Richard be a guest in our house? And if I didn't have a brother, I couldn't be in love with his friend, could I?

I could just take Trish out, but that's kind of hostile. I mean, she'll read the book and wonder why everyone's in it but her. I shouldn't have to be worrying about all this.

I don't want you to think that I'm one of those naive narrators who are the last ones to know what's really happening in a story. I know who my antagonist is as well as you do, and in Chapter Seven she will accelerate her obnoxious behavior, increasing the level of dramatic tension ever so slightly. What are friends for?

I know why Ashley has been my friend. The trouble is I know how this book ends, and I'm not in any mood to give Ashley the benefit of the doubt. Still, I do, sadly, remember why I liked and, yes, *needed* her for my friend. A short list:

1. It was Ashley who allowed me to drop my owly, smart-girl self and entertained me with makeovers. She could do this thing with my eyes using pencils, creams, and little brushes, and suddenly I had dramatic eyes magnified by the glasses. She painted on cheekbones. "You look like Greta Garbo," she'd say in her Greta Garbo voice. And the honest truth is I really do look better with lip gloss.

As long as I can remember, Ashley has had a closet

of costumes—feathery boas, old hats with veils, and gold high heels with straps and glittery bows on top. We'd strut in front of the mirror and call each other Ashley dahling and Kate dahling. For hours at a time, Ashley showed me glamour. I will miss that.

2. She introduced me to trashy television, trashy reading, and trashy food, all of which I loved. Last year we watched *Geraldo* every afternoon. "An hour with dysfunctional people is so invigorating," Ashley would say. "It makes me feel so emotionally stable. I think I'm turning into Joyce Brothers!" We criticized Geraldo's mannerisms—"He strokes his own chest, he's so proud of himself"—and laughed while stuffing down pounds of cheese puffs.

And, of course, those romance novels, which I didn't *have* to read but did, because I, like a voyeur, really liked those three-paragraph, sweat-inducing kisses.

3. Ashley knew how to have fun. If it hadn't been for her, I never would have rented Rollerblades and skated around Lake of the Isles. I never would have spray-painted minor obscenities on the faculty bathroom walls in middle school, the only act of vandalism of my life. I wet my pants, I was so scared. And so thrilled.

She was like having Pandora for a friend. I was never sure what would come out of her box to entertain or horrify me.

Last Christmas I found out what was in the bottom of that box.

* * *

TRISH WAS AT breakfast Christmas Eve morning, but not Bjorn. He had left the house earlier; no one knew where he'd gone. Divorce lawyer would have been my bet.

"I'd like to take individual Christmas portraits of everyone over the next couple of days. Would that be okay with you guys?" Trish spoke shyly, self-consciously. Perhaps she was embarrassed about walking out on us the night before. Perhaps she wondered if we had heard them fighting. I wondered what Mother and Dad had said to them.

"You can take my picture if you'll be kind with the light," my father said, handing her a plate of sausages. He held her shoulder. "This is my good side," he said, tilting his head.

Trish smiled at him.

"I hope you'll take us as a group as well," Mother said.

"You want to remember the Christmas of the invaders?" Fleur was stabbing at a sausage.

"Yes, I do," Mother said.

It was past ten o'clock, because we'd all gotten to bed so late. I wasn't surprised when the back-door bell rang.

"Hello, Ashley," I said, sounding like a school principal. My body blocked the doorway. The freezing air raised goose bumps on my skin immediately.

"Guess what?" she squealed. "I found the diamond earrings! My mother had them hidden in a drawer in the laundry room. They look *gorgeous* on me."

"Great," I mumbled. Ashley had never once been surprised on Christmas day. Manipulators don't like surprises.

83

"Can I come in?" She glanced over my shoulder.

"We're in the middle of breakfast," I said, trying to keep from shivering. I folded my arms for warmth.

"Are you mad at me?" She seemed truly shocked.

"Well, yes, as a matter of fact." I was glad suddenly to be six feet tall, looking down my nose.

"Because of what I said yesterday? I was just being honest." She tried to peer over my shoulder.

"And now I'm being honest. You're just using me to get to Rich when you know—you *know*"—I lowered my voice—"that I like Rich. I thought you were my friend." I was shivering hard now, and suddenly I was afraid I would cry. The cold made it worse. Expressing my disappointment out loud made it worse.

"Kate, close the door, you're freezing us out in here." Mother appeared in the doorway. "Hi, Ashley, come in and join us for breakfast."

Ashley stepped past me into the back hall. "Thanks, Mrs. Bjorkman. Just coffee would be nice."

I closed the door and stood in the hall, hunched over, hugging myself, until I stopped shaking.

"Hi, you guys. Hi, Rich." Ashley's voice grated. The shivering started up again.

As she'd done yesterday morning, she had taken Mother's chair next to Richard and was semihuddled against him. "I'm still cold," she said breathlessly, heaving her breasts under Richard's nose.

He smiled benignly.

"Why don't you put your coat back on?" I said and wished I hadn't. It sounded sullen, the way I felt.

"Do you still want help with your Desdemona paper?" Could Fleur sense my misery?

I nodded.

"Let's run down to the university library the day after Christmas. I don't know how long I'm going to be here after that."

"Aren't you leaving with the others?" I had heard Bjorn say they would leave after New Year's because he wanted Trish to experience New Year's *Eve*. It's a kind of joke in our family.

"I was going to—" She smiled, embarrassed. "I was thinking maybe I should attend my mother's wedding."

"Oh, I forgot." I had wondered last night why she would choose this Christmas to spend in Minnesota if her mother was getting married, but then I figured that a family with parents marrying over and over again operated under different rules.

"Don't say anything to the others." She had lowered her voice. "I haven't made up my mind yet."

I nodded.

The garage door opened, and a few minutes later Bjorn burst into the room with an armload of packages.

"I hope you bought me something small and expensive," I said.

"Diamond earrings!" Ashley said.

Stuff the diamond earrings.

"Have you eaten?" Mother asked.

"No, and I'm starving," Bjorn said.

There wasn't a vacant chair in the room. "Sit here," Richard said, standing. He moved over to the counter to make more pancakes.

85

Ashley looked disappointed.

"I drove past Como Lake this morning." Bjorn's look took in everyone, but Trish got the most repeated glances. "The snowplows have cleaned one section of ice for skating. I thought it might be fun to go—you know—" His eyes shifted again and again to Trish. Hadn't they made up yet? "Go skating. What do you think?"

"I've never been ice-skating." Fleur made it sound like bungee-jumping.

Richard turned away from the frying pan. "That's why you came, isn't it? To *experience* winter?"

"No, I think it's great. Let's do it."

"Fleur and I don't have any skates," Trish said.

"I'm sure we can find some around," Mother said.

"If not, there's a place where you can rent them," Bjorn was quick to add.

"I'll bring some cocoa in a thermos for everyone." Ashley had found a way to be included.

MOTHER HAD FOUND skates that fit Trish and Fleur and was wiping them off in the front hall when she saw a boy carrying a large white box tied with a red ribbon walking up the front steps. "What's this?" She opened the door before he had a chance to ring the doorbell.

"Delivery for Ms. Trish Bjorkman?" the boy said.

"Trish?" Mother turned.

"For me?" Trish rose from the stairs where she'd been sitting. She signed the receipt and took the long box from the boy. "Merry Christmas!" she called to him as he hurried down the walk. Her voice was the cheeriest I'd heard it in the last twenty-four hours.

She lifted the lid and folded back the tissue paper. "Oh, oh, how beautiful, how exquisite!" She leaned her face into the box to smell the roses.

Fleur picked up the card that had fallen to the floor and handed it to Trish. "Bet they're not from Santa Claus," she said, lips pursed.

"What's holding up this show?" Richard came in from the kitchen, followed by Bjorn, who was working hard to keep his face neutral.

Trish, having read the note, swung on Bjorn, embracing him with her one free arm. "Of course I forgive you." She kissed his lips. "Bjorn, they're so beautiful." She kissed him again. "I've never had such a lovely gift. Thank you!" Kiss. Kiss. Kiss. Smooch. Smooch.

Bjorn had his arms around her. "Things okay now?"

"Yes, I love you so much." Smooch again.

Mother, with a tight-lipped smile, was already on her way to the kitchen. "You'll need a vase," she said.

Something was wrong with this picture, but what? I felt exactly the way I had felt in Sims Market a few nights before, when Ashley and Kirk had "performed" in front of me. The roses were lovely and, yes, romantic. Trish was happy. Bjorn was happy. Why this feeling of mine? Perhaps it was that I was acutely aware that Mother thought a dozen roses were a profound cliché. She had said this many times. "A dozen lilies are far better." Mother's voice was loud in my head. Hadn't Bjorn heard her say it?

87

He and Trish followed Mother into the kitchen, clinging to each other.

Fleur heaved what seemed to me a disgusted sigh. "Forgot my gloves." She ran upstairs.

Richard stood at the edge of the dining room watching me, his hands in his coat pockets. "Bribery seems to be a strong aphrodisiac," he said.

Bribery?

"I guess," I said. I followed Fleur up the stairs for a second pair of wool socks in case I got cold.

In my bedroom, Fleur was ripping at her hair with a hairbrush. As usual, our eyes locked in the mirror. She stopped brushing. "Roses don't solve anything. It's just a bribe to get her to be nice to him again. My mother fell for it all the time. Geez." She set the brush on the chest and turned around to face me directly. Her expression softened. "I'm sorry. Bjorn's your brother—I have no right—"

My hand fluttered up. "No, it's okay. In fact, Richard just called it a bribe too." I didn't quite understand. If Bjorn and Trish were now speaking to each other, wasn't that a good thing?

Fleur read my thoughts. "The roses were a nice gesture, really. But they need to talk about how they're going to make decisions when they don't agree."

Then lilies, I thought, even though they're not a cliché, would have been a bribe too. They just would have been in better taste (according to Mother). Love was confusing. Even dangerous. I had sensed this when the roses arrived and Trish had forgiven Bjorn so easily.

I believed Fleur, but I couldn't help thinking that I would like a dozen roses or lilies from Richard. Or just a nod.

"Maybe they need marriage counseling," I said. Depressing to think about.

"Years of it," Fleur said. "Come on, let's go. They'll be waiting."

Downstairs Ashley had returned with a thermos of hot chocolate, and we were on our way, finally. Fleur, Ashley, and I shared the middle seat this time, because Richard had offered to sit in the very back. I saw Ashley struggling with the notion of getting in the back with him, but she sat with us girls.

Even though it was well below zero, the weather was perfect: blue sky and no wind. Pristine white snow crystallized the trees, which glinted in the sun. The ice rink was jammed with people, all of them well muffled against the cold.

"Looks like everybody in St. Paul had the same idea today," Richard said as we entered the warming house. We changed into our skates and headed for the ice. Trish knew how to skate, and she and Bjorn sped into the crowd holding hands.

"I think I'm going to regret this," Fleur said. She walked stiffly, elbows out.

"Come on," Richard said, taking her hand. "Just keep your ankles vertical." They stepped onto the ice.

Richard laughed quietly. "You have to move your feet, Fleur!"

She stood rigid. A tiny kid, almost a toddler, whizzed past her on miniature skates.

"Why?" Fleur demanded.

"Otherwise it's not skating." He tugged at her arm. "Relax," he said.

She grasped Richard's arm with both hands, and he more or less pulled her around the ice like a tugboat pulling the dead weight of an ocean liner. "Move your feet!" he yelled and then laughed.

Ashley stood by me, squinting in the bright sun, watching the two of them.

"What exactly is their relationship, I wonder." She looked at me.

"They're secretly married, I think." I shoved off onto the ice.

"Very funny," she called after me.

It looked like an ordinary friendship to me, but it baffled me. Fleur was the most beautiful and likable girl I'd ever met and Richard was—well, he was Richard. How could they resist each other? I didn't know anything.

I skated alone mostly. Ashley found Mike Nelson, a guy from school, and skated with him for a long while. She was animated and sexy—I could see it. She kept glancing at Richard to see if he noticed her with Mike, but he never did.

Trish and Bjorn were completely enchanted with each other—the magic of roses and all. Fleur was right. No decision had been made about future Christmas tree purchases. The roses seemed like a cheap reconciliation. Bah humbug.

"Why so grim?" Richard came out of nowhere and took my arm.

"I don't ever want roses to soothe over a fight." I said it out loud. I hadn't meant to.

His eyebrows rose and he looked at me in "amused wonder," as the phrase book says. "I'll just include that on my list," he said, a smile edging his lips.

"I mean—" *What do you mean, birdbrain?* "I mean I would prefer directness." Brilliant.

"It takes two people to be direct."

"I always am." Was that self-righteous tone coming from *my* mouth? I hoped he hadn't noticed.

He smirked. "Were you being direct yesterday when you walked blindly about without your glasses?" He pulled me aside a little to keep a kid from skating into me.

I felt my face flush. That's what I got for listening to someone as transparent as Ashley.

I attacked him with both fists. "You don't know anything, *Mr. Man!*"

He warded off my blows, laughing, and, finally catching my fists, held them. "Did I say something wrong, *Ms. Woman?* Tell me I'm wrong. Come on," he said, pulling me along the ice. "Everyone's in the warming house having cocoa."

We held hands as we headed across the rink. I thought I would explode with joy.

"I think we should come skating early tomorrow morning before breakfast," he said.

"Christmas morning?"

"No one will be here; we'll have the place to ourselves. Might be nice, don't you think?"

Did he mean just the two of us? My pulse quickened. "Sure," I said.

"Good. I'll ask everyone."

I smiled secretly at my foolishness.

We joined the others in a corner of the warming house.

"Here's yours." Ashley was quick to hand Richard his mug. "It has amaretto in it." Had she always been so transparent, or had I been brain-dead these past ten years?

Fleur handed me a mug and made room for me on the bench.

"How do you like ice-skating?" I asked her.

"Frankly, I hate it," she said. She reached down and rubbed one of her ankles.

"Boo and I were thinking—" Richard began.

"We were just talking about Aunt Eve's dinner-dance," Ashley cut in.

I knew what was coming. Ashley was going to go for the jugular right now, here in the warming house, and it would work for her as it always did. I knew what was coming even before she invited Richard out for New Year's Eve.

"You're going, aren't you?" She was speaking to Bjorn.

He nodded. "Wouldn't miss it. I want Trish to see the Pink Palace—the Hearst Castle of Lake Minnetonka." He grinned.

"Fantasyland," Richard agreed.

"I'd really like you to be my partner," Ashley said to Richard.

Richard spilled cocoa on himself. "Uh," he said. He looked at me for help.

"I think Mother was expecting Rich to take Fleur," I said.

"Fleur is flying home *before* New Year's Eve," Ashley announced grandly.

I looked at Fleur. "I decided to go to the wedding after all."

"Good," Richard and I said together.

"I thought you asked Kirk," I said to Ashley.

"He can't go," Ashley said quickly. "Will you go with me?" she asked Richard again, keeping her voice light.

I don't know why, but Richard looked at me again. "Are you going?" he asked.

"She's going with Helmut Weiss, so they can discuss transformational grammar." Satisfaction on her smug face.

I sighed. "Helmut is good company, Ashley." Which was more than I could say for her.

"You will go, won't you?" Ashley fluttered the eyelashes. Gag, gag, and throw up.

"Well." Richard recovered himself. "Sure," he said to Ashley. "That'll be fun."

"Oh good," she said. "Have some more cocoa." She poured some from the thermos into his cup. "Do you want more, Kate?"

Pushing my glasses back on my nose, I shook my head. I'd had enough poison for one day.

* * *

In the afternoon, Fleur and Richard went shopping. Bjorn took Trish to meet some of his old friends.

I helped Mother set the table for dinner in the dining room and then, turning on the tree lights, lay wrapped in a Christmas quilt, which my mother brought out every year, on the sofa in the living room. From Dad's study came the strains of "All We like Sheep" from the *Messiah*. I hummed softly along, while "a bitter cold despair dwelt in the caves of my lonely soul." A quote from *The Romance Writer's Phrase Book*. Really! Does anyone in America talk that way? Caves of my lonely soul?

But I was sad about the disparity between reality and fantasy where Richard was concerned. "Am I wrong?" he had asked, teasing me on the stairs that morning. Am I wrong to think you like me? That's what he was asking.

Does it make a difference?

I felt sad that my friendship with Ashley was over. I had been an expendable sidekick to her. Me Tonto.

Mother stood in the archway. "Tea?"

I nodded.

She left and returned with a steaming cup on a saucer—the good china—and a red linen napkin. I sat up, my legs still stretched out on the sofa. She sat by my feet, rubbing them through the wool socks. "Merry Christmas," she said.

"Merry Christmas, best mother of mine." I smiled. The steam from the tea fogged my glasses. "I need windshield wipers," I said, looking at her through the mist.

She nodded.

The tea, hot and strong, along with my mother massaging my feet and Handel's music wafting from Dad's study, loosened something in me. Something that had been tight. Something I had kept hidden but that now surfaced. Tears unexpectedly burned at the edges of my eyelids. I blinked them back. The tree lights blurred. It's funny how sometimes the smallest unexpected kindness—my mother rubbing my feet, for example—can call forth the most hidden sadness.

I sipped the hot tea. "I wish I were beautiful," I said.

Mother smoothed the corduroy against my leg. I loved her for not trying to argue me out of anything. She pulled on the hem of the slacks.

"I just wish I were beautiful."

She sat with me until the afternoon turned gray, until the oven timer went off and she had to finish the Christmas Eve dinner in the kitchen.

THE TRADITIONAL CHRISTMAS EVE dinner at our house is an authentic Swedish smorgasbord that my mother spreads out across the buffet in silver and fine china. There are, of course, meatballs made with sausage and ham, cheese, at least three kinds of pickled herring, a pork roast, lutefisk with white sauce, and saffron buns. The dining room is lit with candles only—candles on the buffet and on the table, and candles in a spectacular wreath of greens, especially mistletoe, that my father suspends over the dining room table from the ceiling with wide red ribbon just before dinner. It is our family's nod to the Festival of Lights. The wreath is the width of the dining table—my mother's design. Fleur and Trish oohed and aahed when they saw it for the first time. They had come

95

down the stairs dressed to the teeth. I didn't look bad either. Mother had said earlier, "Wear what makes you comfortable," but Bjorn had interpreted: "She likes us dressed up."

"But not uncomfortably dressed up," Mother had said.

"No formal wear," Bjorn had interpreted.

Mother had turned from the kitchen sink, where she was washing her hands, and, purposely splattering water on Bjorn, said, "Am I not speaking English?"

All the men wore jackets and ties. My stomach curled when I saw Richard in a charcoal-tweed coat with a crisp blue oxford shirt. Silent sighing and accelerated pulse all over the place.

"When did that gorgeous wreath go up?" Trish wanted to know.

"Don't know," Dad said. "Keebler elves." He kissed her cheek. "Mistletoe." He pointed at the wreath.

Soon everyone was kissing. Trish and Fleur kissed Dad on each cheek at the same time. "Merry Christmas, Professor Bjorkman," Fleur said, grinning. His ears colored shamelessly. Mother passed out drinks and received kisses from all the men.

Bjorn smacked a wet one on my nose, followed by another wet one on my cheek. "Like being kissed by a Saint Bernard." I laughed and, turning, faced Richard.

He raised his glass to mine. "Merry Christmas, Kate," he said, using my name for the first time. He kissed me lightly, gently, on the lips. Our eyes held.

"Merry Christmas, Richard," I said and, catching myself, said, "I mean Rich."

"I like Richard," he said.

"I like Kate."

He smiled. "I'll try to remember," he said, and he kissed me ever so lightly again. "Kate."

I thought I would melt into the carpet.

Mother encouraged us to try everything. Trish passed up all three varieties of herring, but Bjorn spooned some on her plate along with chopped onions. "The Swedes call it *sill*," he said. He also spooned a little lutefisk on her plate. "Cod," he said. He didn't say anything about the lye marinade. "You'll love it."

Fleur was interested in all the food, asking Mother if various dishes were hard to make, if she'd thought of writing a Christmas cookbook.

"I'm sure it's all been done," Mother said.

"No," Fleur said. "Not just food recipes, but directions for making the wreath, for all the homemade things you have to decorate the house—all of it."

"You think it would work?" Mother asked.

Dad and Richard talked graduate schools. "You want to continue in comp. lit.?" Dad asked.

Richard shook his head. "American studies," he said, ladling Swedish meatballs from the chafing dish.

"Well then, Minnesota ought to be a consideration."

"It is."

"Good," Dad said.

The thought that Richard might move back to Minnesota raised powerful emotions in me. I had not even thought about going to the University of Minnesota. I wanted to go to school in the East, but if Richard was coming home, then I was staying here for school. Only

The Romance Writer's Phrase Book could describe my feelings in the chapter on emotions, under the subheading "Happiness, Joy." Here's a list: (1) *Joy bubbled in her laugh and shone in her eyes.* (2) *She felt a bottomless peace and satisfaction.* (3) *Tonight there were no shadows across her heart.* (4) *Her heart sang with delight.* (5) *She was blissfully happy, fully alive.* And my favorite: (6) *She was wrapped in a silken cocoon of euphoria.*

We had the traditional rice pudding for dessert, and Fleur almost broke a tooth on the almond hidden in her serving.

"Oh, I forgot to warn you!" Mother looked truly sorry. "There's always an almond hidden in the pudding, and whoever gets it will be married in the next year."

Fleur removed the almond from her mouth and set it delicately on the edge of her plate. "No way," she said.

"Take it home to your mother," I said.

"She must run into almonds in everything she eats," Fleur said.

After dinner Mother brought out a basket of tiny presents wrapped in glossy red-and-green paper. "There's one for everyone," she said. We opened them to find colored metal windup bugs. Mine was a ladybug, Richard's a spider, Trish's a grasshopper, Bjorn's a beetle, and so on. We wound them up and let them crawl around the table and then raced them and ran them into each other.

"Ideas like this should go into the cookbook too," Fleur told Mother.

"Are you going to help?" Mother asked.

"Absolutely," Fleur said.

Later in the living room, Dad read the Christmas story from the King James Bible. I sat next to him, my head resting on his shoulder. Once in a while I would look up to find Richard considering me from across the room. Maybe it was wishful thinking. No, his lips compressed into a definite smile.

Richard and Bjorn wanted to go to midnight Mass at the Cathedral of St. Paul. They weren't Catholic, but they wanted to sit in the cathedral, one of St. Paul's grandest landmarks.

Mother hesitated—there was so much to clean up, she said. But we said we'd do the cleaning up for her and Dad, since they—especially Mother—had prepared the meal. They agreed to go. We crowded together in a pew on the far side near the back. Across the aisle I saw Mr. Sims, his fingers nervously tapping the prayer book in his lap. He seemed to be there alone. I smiled at him, but he was too caught up in his own thoughts to notice. There had been a Mrs. Sims, I was sure of it. I thought of the Midgelys, who had had happier Christmas Eves in the past, and I knew that, life being what it was, "the full spectrum of tragedy and comedy," as Midgely had said, this night with my family and with friends who felt like family was a gift, and I said a silent prayer of gratitude.

Revision Notes

I got so excited to be able to write about Richard kissing me lightly on Christmas Eve and calling me Kate that I rushed through the chapter, forgetting an important scene with Fleur. I'm going to have to go back and stick it in. It happened before the kiss, before dinner.

We were up in my bedroom dressing for dinner. That is, she was dressing, and I was trying on everything I owned and rejecting each outfit. It didn't help that Fleur wore this glittery white beaded sweater that made her look like Aphrodite or one of those other spell-casting goddesses.

"This isn't any good either," I said, throwing down a cream silk dress that normally looked wonderful on me but not that night. My bed was piled high with discards.

"This is great!" Fleur said, retrieving the dress.

"Mother brought the material back from India and had it made up for me." My voice was sullen and defeated. I sat on the bed in my underwear. "Might as well go down like this."

Fleur turned and seemed to see me for the first time that evening. "Who are you dressing for? You're so nervous."

"Nobody." It came out in a squeak. "That is—Mother likes us to look nice. I—I—"

Fleur pulled on her nose. "Wrong, but thank you for playing."

I smiled. "It's all the company, I guess—"

"Me? I'm the only one you didn't know already."

"Oh no, not you—I like you—you're terrific. It's just th-that—" Stammer, stammer. "I'm having my period." It was a lie but a good one. I smiled, pleased.

Fleur held the cream dress up to herself in front of the mirror. Her back was toward me, but I saw her face reflected. "I think," she said, "that Rich really likes you. I mean, really, really likes you."

I was on my feet, dancing back and forth. "No way," I said. "I think he likes *you*." I grabbed the silk dress from her. "This is good enough. I'll wear this." And struggled into it as fast as I could, glad to hide my searing face in the fabric for a few seconds.

When I emerged, Fleur's mouth gaped broadly. "Me and Rich? Are you hallucinating?"

"You're such an obvious match." I buttoned buttons, relieved not to have to look at her. "I'm glad you two are dating. I like you and I've always liked Rich." I searched in the closet for the belt to the dress.

"Believe me," Fleur said, "I am not dating *Mr. Radio*. We're just friends."

"Mr. Radio? Rich?"

"Haven't you heard us call him that?"

"No."

"Haven't you seen how he always seems to have just the right thing to say—"

"I don't see anything wrong with—"

"There isn't. It's just that sometimes—you know—he's so *smooth*. Like a radio announcer."

Or like a used-car salesman?

Fleur handed me the belt I needed. "I don't mean anything negative by it. It's just the way Rich is: golden-throated, glib. You know."

"I would just say he was articulate."

Fleur smiled at me. "You like Rich a lot, don't you?"

I felt as if I were in a movie—*The Sound of Music*. I was Maria, and Fleur was the baroness. That bedroom scene, only I couldn't escape to the abbey and Mother Superior. "I can't like him when you're dating him," I said. The faulty logic did not escape me.

Fleur grabbed me by the shoulders. "We're not dating. We've never dated. We're really just friends. Honest."

She looked honest enough. In the mirror I could see that my buttons were in the wrong holes. I looked insane. "Then why did you come with him? Why are you here?"

"Because for years Bjorn and Rich have been talking about this neighborhood and their families. It sounded idyllic. I wanted to see it for myself. I wanted to meet your parents and you. I wanted to see this block, this house."

I must have looked skeptical, because she added, "Do you know that I don't know any parents who have stayed married until their children were grown? Not one couple. Your family seems magical to me." Her head lowered. Was she going to cry?

"Don't you think we're boring?"

"If that's boring, I envy it." Then she saw my buttons and

laughed. "I don't think you really want to wear that dress," she said.

When we went downstairs, I was wearing a white beaded sweater that made me feel like a glittering goddess and Fleur was dressed in a cream silk dress that came almost to her ankles. Her generosity was the kind of gesture I had hoped for from Ashley.

Are you ready for the three-paragraph kiss? It happens in this chapter, Chapter Eight. In *The Romance Writer's Phrase Book*, "Kisses" is a subheading in the chapter on sex, which is the second-longest chapter in the book, the chapter on emotions being the longest. I suppose this is because the entire romance novel is a description of emotions punctuated by three-paragraph kisses and, in many cases, lovemaking. Don't get your hopes up, though. There is no lovemaking in this book.

While cleaning up the dishes after Mass the night before, Richard persuaded everyone to go skating before breakfast Christmas morning, even Mother and Dad. Even Fleur, who at the initial suggestion said, "Let's not, and say we did."

We agreed to go at seven.

I was glad Richard had been cut off with this idea earlier in the day in the warming house, by Ashley no less, because now she wouldn't be there.

Which all brings me to this: have you ever had one of those times when you knew that the gods, or in my case goddesses, were on your side? A time when the stars and planets converged to make things happen your way? A time when, like a gypsy, you could see the immediate future with a startling clarity? And it was good?

It happened that way early Christmas morning. Even before I put on my glasses, I knew that Richard and I would be the only ones going skating. I knew that no matter how much I cajoled Fleur and shook her and promised her coffee, she would not get up.

And I was not surprised, when stepping out into the hallway, to hear Bjorn from behind a narrow opening in his door telling Richard that he and Trish were too tired to go.

"Wimps," Richard said softly as Bjorn closed the door.

"Same here," Mother said, leaning her head out of their bedroom door. "Do you mind very much?"

"You deserve a rest," Richard said, smiling.

She blew him a kiss and shut the door quietly.

Already knowing the future, I could afford to say, "Fleur refuses to wake up. Would you rather not go?"

He put his arm around my shoulder, his fingers lightly touching my neck, and guided me toward the stairs. "Two is still company," he said.

I wondered if I should have worn lip gloss.

There was coffee brewing in the coffeemaker, which we poured into a thermos; then we started a fresh pot for the others.

Out in the garage, Richard's eyes landed on the convertible. "Let's take *it*," he said. "With the top down."

I pushed the garage door opener. "I'll get the keys."

Strains of one of Dad's favorite Christmas melodies, "In dulci jubilo"—Praetorius, I think—welled inside me. I hummed it finding the keys, hummed it pulling two quilts out of the linen closet. It was Christmas morning. I was a brass ensemble.

We drove, top down, windows up, folded blankets on our laps, the heater struggling to warm our feet. We drove, giggling at our "one-horse open sleigh," as Richard called it, past Ashley's house. I wished she could see me now.

The warming house was closed, the park not officially open until nine. We changed into our skates at the edge of the ice, wrapping our boots in one of the quilts. The thermos of coffee we wrapped in the second quilt.

I followed Richard out onto the ice, which had the barest dusting of snow on it. "Isn't it great?" he said, making a wide sweep across the rink, while I repeated figure eights in the center. The morning was gray, the sun not yet above the horizon.

"My favorite Christmas was spent here." He was skating alongside me now. "It was when I was five." His breath appeared in hot bursts of little clouds in front of his mouth.

I wished I could remember Richard at five. "Here?"

He nodded. "The year I got my first pair of hockey skates, black, like my dad's."

We had skated around the edge of the rink and now cut through the center.

"He brought me here right after we opened the presents and it was like this—like now—just the two of us on the ice, and he gave me my first skating lesson."

His elbow nudged me slightly, directing me out of the center to the left.

"You must have been good at it right away. I hated my first skating lesson." I was beginning to puff a little.

"I don't know. It was just nice, you know, to be alone with my dad." He colored slightly.

"Without Melissa there to call the shots?" Melissa was his older sister.

"You got it." We had quite naturally taken a couple's position holding left hands in front, his right arm around my waist, right hands clasped at the side. We skated faster, more uniformly that way, cutting wide sweeps of eights. It was fun to skate with him. He was taller than I was, for one thing, a rarity in my case. We shared a kind of synchronized rhythm. Sometimes when you skate with a guy, you're always bumping hips and elbows, colliding, and nothing can fix it. Richard and I glided easily, anticipating corners, leaning together.

"So this is a nostalgic visit for you—this trip," I prodded. *Tell me about your life. Share with me. Treat me like one of the grown-ups.*

"I guess. Let's try one of those backward moves, you know, as we come out of the top of the eight," he said. "Are you game?"

"Sure—you mean to the left and back?"

He nodded. "And then I'll swing around—you're the pivot point, or whatever they call it."

We skated the edge of the circle and swept up the middle, then left, backward, around, and then backward again, and around, and one more time.

"Hey," he cried. "We're good together!"

Damn right.

"Let's try waltz position," he suggested. We rearranged ourselves and began cautiously. "I learned how to skate in waltz position from Skeeter Dicou, the hockey coach in middle school, believe it or not. Bjorn was my partner."

"Romantic," I said.

We swirled easily. It was like dancing in a dream.

"We hated it, but old Dicou said we had to be absolutely flexible." He laughed. "That was his favorite word —flexible." He skated backward now, pulling me along with him. "I'm talking too much," he said.

"I like the stories." Our cold, smoky breaths mingled and dissipated.

"You tell me one, then."

I tried not to flinch from his direct gaze. "*My* favorite Christmas was the year we got Ruffy."

He began laughing. "I'd like to hear *your* version; I've heard Bjorn's."

"Well, Ruffy was in my stocking. His little baggy beagle face hung over the edge just so, panting." I imitated Ruffy's panting. It pleased me to entertain Richard. "He couldn't have been in that stocking all that long. I'm sure Dad stuffed him in there just before Bjorn and I came downstairs."

He nodded, grinning. Beyond his shoulder, a pink glow appeared on the horizon. A couple of cars, the first we'd seen, drove east on the boulevard. He pulled me closer and swung me around sharply.

"Tricky," I said, but we pulled it off nicely. "Anyway, I

was ecstatic to see that dog in my stocking, and he was obviously *very excited* to meet me."

Richard shook with suppressed laughter.

"He was *very, very excited* to meet me. He licked my face and when I put him down, he danced around my feet and begged me to pick him up again—"

"You speak doggie?"

"Of course. Well, then Mother reminded me that there were other things in my stocking besides that dog. So I reached into the stocking and my hand sank into something warm, wet, and putrid—dog doo!"

"Bjorn uses a different vocabulary."

"Whatever you call it, it was disgusting. I screamed my head off, but in the end it was still my favorite Christmas."

"I remember the Christmas you got Ruffy for similar reasons, actually."

"He peed on you when you picked him up!"

"You remember?"

I remember everything about you, I thought. I said, "Mother made you take off your pants, so she could wash them. You sat in the kitchen—that was before it was remodeled—"

"In her wraparound apron in front of the stove," he finished.

"She probably made you drink Russian tea."

"No, she gave me hot chocolate with extra whipped cream."

I saw him as if it were yesterday sitting on one of the old kitchen chairs we used to have, holding the Santa Claus mug in his hands. "Don't come in here, Katie," he had yelled at me when I stood in the doorway. "Go away."

And I had asked Mother, "Are you washing his underpants too?"

I must have smiled, because Richard asked now, "What are you thinking?"

"I was still wondering if you were wearing underpants under that apron," I said, laughing.

It was then, as we twirled at the edge of the ice close to the snowbank, that my skate caught on a bump in the ice and, losing my balance, I fell against Richard, who struggled for a few brief seconds to keep us vertical but failed. We crashed to the ice, limbs flailing in all directions.

"Are you okay?" Richard hovered over me.

"My glasses—" The whole world seemed hidden behind a gray, gauzy film. I heard a car on the road above us but could not see it, not even a shadow. "I can't see."

He twisted around. "Oh geez," he said. He reached in back of him and, turning, handed me my glasses. "I'm sorry," he said.

One sidepiece had completely broken off, and the other was badly twisted. Knowing better, I tried to straighten it, and it snapped off in my hands. Luckily the frames and the lenses were almost intact. One lens had a deep crack running through it. "From glasses to pince-nez," I said to Richard, who still crouched over me. "Do you think it's an improvement?" I tried to balance the frames on my nose, but they fell into my lap.

"Can you see anything without them?" he asked.

I looked into his face, which was inches from mine. "You," I said. "I can see you."

I don't know if it was the fact that I wasn't wearing my glasses just then, and I was prettier without them, that moved him to kiss me—that would have been Ashley's reasoning—or if it was that he had wanted to kiss me all morning, glasses or no glasses, or if it was simply impulsive. Richard kissed me. "Kate," he said, his lips grazing mine as he spoke. Then his mouth closed down on mine, but it was not, as the phrase book says, "like soldering heat that joins metals." It was warm like summer. And he did not, as the phrase book says, take my mouth "with a savage intensity," nor did he "smother" my lips "with demanding mastery," nor did he "devour" me, nor was it a "punishing kiss." I wouldn't have liked any of that macho stuff. His hands—when had he removed his gloves?—held my face, and I reached up and held his wrist. It was like summer, his kiss was. Have I said that?

Frankly, I'm finding that writing a three-paragraph kiss is difficult—impossible, maybe. I'm thinking that what it felt like explicitly and where our tongues were explicitly and that usual kind of three-paragraph detail is none of your damn business.

The phrase book is right: I did "breathe lightly between parted lips" when it was over. We grinned at each other, a little foolishly, maybe. He pulled me up to my feet.

So now it's time for the full-body kiss, because his arms did slip around me easily, drawing me in, and I wound my arms around his neck. He kissed my hair; I

111

kissed his face, which smelled of soap, and then, "reclaiming her lips, he crushed her to him."

Even if that were true, I could never write such a thing. Even if his touch *was* "divine ecstasy," even if the warmth of him *was* "intoxicating," even if my body *was* "tingling," I couldn't write that. It sounds stupid.

I can tell you another thing: he did not "lift me into the cradle of his arms." I'm six feet tall, for pity's sake!

And though we were smashed together in a pleasing way, my "soft curves" were not "molded to the contours of his lean body." This *was* Minnesota in December. We had so many clothes on, we might as well have been steel-belted radial tires.

I don't mean to put it down. It was delicious kissing Richard. I was born to kiss him. I just don't want to talk it to death.

We parted, reluctantly. "I could spend all day here," he said, his lips on my hair.

"I don't want to go back either."

"You think they'd wonder if we didn't show up?"

"I think they'd call the police."

Our lips touched lightly. "Mmm." I don't know who said it. "Mmm."

He took my hand and led me back to the place where we had left our boots and the thermos of coffee. I held my glasses up to my eyes to keep from getting dizzy. We sat down on a bench close to the ice, with the quilt that had protected the thermos covering our legs. Richard poured coffee into the thermos cup. "We forgot an extra cup," he said. "We'll have to share, cooties and all." He grinned.

"It's a little late for worrying about cooties." I sipped the coffee, which was still hot.

We passed the cup back and forth. He poured more coffee from the thermos. "I couldn't go to Bjorn's wedding last summer," he began, holding the cup in his lap, his long slender fingers folded around it. "I had a Fulbright to study in Germany."

"I know. It happened pretty fast," I said. I was twisted toward him, my arm propped up against the back of the bench, my glasses secure in my lap. He was all I wanted to see anyway. I remembered being disappointed when I found out Richard wasn't going to be there to be Bjorn's best man.

"In the fall, when I got back, Bjorn, of course, showed me the wedding pictures." He looked down into the coffee and then at me. "And there *you* were looking—I mean, I was expecting pigtails and—"

"Dead mice?"

He grinned. "Maybe. I expected to see Bjorn's *little* sister—"

"Boo?"

He nodded. "Yeah, *that* little sister. I think I always had a little crush on you—"

"No, no. I was the one who had the crush!"

"Anyway"—he sipped the coffee—"when I saw the pictures, I wanted to see you, Kate."

That's when the sun lifted above the horizon, sending silver rays glinting across the ice, and a chorus of angels descended in a cloud, glitter in their hair, singing, "Gloria, glorissima." Or perhaps it was one of those hallucinations. My glasses were in my lap, after all. But

Richard Bradshaw had come to see me. *Moi.* We did a lot more kissing.

We pulled apart when a car stopped above us and the doors opened and shut. Richard turned to look. "The police." He grinned.

I held my glasses in front of my eyes. It was a small boy and his dad.

"Will you hold on to me?" the boy asked. He carried brand-new skates.

"You bet," his dad said.

I watched Richard. "What goes around, comes around," I mused.

"Come on," he said, screwing the lid onto the thermos. "Let's let them have the place to themselves."

The rest of Christmas day, which is Chapter Nine, continued with an embarrassment of riches, emotionally speaking. When we got home, everyone sat around the kitchen table eating Danish (or "Swedish," as my father calls them) with coffee. They were a disheveled-looking bunch, still in pajamas. I liked it. They looked like a family.

"What in the world happened to your glasses?" Mother asked. I was holding them up to my face with both hands.

"We fell down and so did the glasses," I said.

"I can only waltz with Bjorn," Richard said.

"No, no, he's a great skater," I said. "My skate caught on the ice—"

"There's snow all over your hair. Was it snowing?" Mother asked.

"It just started a few minutes ago. It's snowing really hard now," I said, brushing the top of my head. I began laughing, helplessly. I've been kissing Richard, I thought.

Richard, who must have been thinking just about the

same thing, grinned. "We took the convertible with the top down—hope you don't mind. There's only a little snow in it."

"You and Boo went skating alone?" Bjorn's credulity was stretched. "In the convertible?"

"*Kate* and I went skating alone in the convertible," Richard corrected. His arm went around my shoulder. "And we had a terrific time." He was owning me as an equal in front of Bjorn—in front of everyone. My face flushed with satisfaction.

"Yes, terrific about covers it," I said.

Mother looked at Dad. Bjorn looked at Trish. Fleur locked eyes with me as usual, a funny smile curving her lips.

"I don't think we were missed," Dad muttered.

"Something's going on," Bjorn said.

"Good guess, Einstein." Trish patted the top of his head.

"Any Danish left? I'm starving," I said.

"Me too," Richard said.

Mother passed us the plate of Danish. "Take two."

WE DIDN'T OPEN presents until everyone had showered and changed.

Richard gave me a volume of Dylan Thomas and changed the inscription in the front immediately, crossing out "Boo" and writing in "Kate," lengthening "Rich" to "Richard," and adding "With love." "It needed revising," he said, handing it back to me.

He liked the book on the Boundary Waters a lot.

"Let's go on a canoe trip next summer." He was looking straight at me. "You want to?"

Bjorn, who was pulling a new sweater over his head, said, "Great idea! We could drive to the end of the Gunflint Trail, leave our car at—"

Trish tugged at his sweater. "I don't think you've been invited." She laughed.

"You're kidding." He looked like a hurt puppy.

I burst out laughing. "Let him come, Richard," I said. "Let the big baby come."

Then I got chased around the house by Bjorn, who made wild threats to lock me in my room until I was thirty.

The rest of the morning passed peacefully. Dad had gotten fly-tying equipment, as well as a new fly rod—a Sage, which is supposed to be superimpressive but looked like anything you could get at Target or Wal-Mart. When he learned that Richard had been tying his own flies for years, he attached the vise to the dining room table and made Richard teach him how to make "woolly buggers."

Fleur and Mother sat together in the kitchen poring over recipes for the Christmas cookbook. Fleur said she would be the guinea pig and try all the recipes this spring. "That way," she said, "if some instruction isn't clear, we can revise the recipe."

I wondered if she wouldn't like having my mother for a mother. The idea made me sad.

I sat on the sofa and read some Dylan Thomas, but between having to hold up my glasses and having to read through the crack in one lens, it was easier to do nothing but listen to the English carols playing on the stereo. Once I brought my glasses up to my face to look across the room into the dining room at Richard's dark head next to my father's, bent over the vise. Would I dislike him one day? Would I throw a blender at him? His head shot up unexpectedly. Our eyes held across the space of two rooms. "Merry Christmas," he called. My dad glanced back and forth at Richard and me and bent back down to finish the stone fly he was trying for the first time.

"Merry Christmas," I said. Throw a blender at that head? Never.

I must have fallen asleep, because I didn't hear the doorbell ring, didn't hear Ashley come into the room. It was as if I awoke in her midsentence almost. She was showing me her new diamond earrings. "They're one carat each," she squealed. "From Hudson's." Her voice was too loud, the inflections too exaggerated. She was playing to Richard in the other room.

"Wait." I felt disoriented and then, realizing my glasses were in my lap, held them up to my face. "They're lovely," I said. I wondered how her mother, a kindergarten teacher, could possibly afford two carats of diamonds. Ashley must have really pushed her to her limits. "And I got this new dress I wanted too." She had brought it with her in a Dayton's shopping bag, a beaded burgundy two-piece dress. She held it against herself after making sure to move out of Richard's line of vision. Not that it mattered. He wasn't interested. He and Dad crouched together over the table, tying impossible knots with nearly invisible thread.

"It's stunning," I said, and I wasn't lying.

She folded it back into the bag and whispered, "I'm wearing it on New Year's Eve. I really hit the jackpot this year."

Did she mean with Christmas presents or with Richard as her date for New Year's or both?

"Santa Claus must have struck it rich." My head had been on the sofa pillow, but now I sat up.

"Oh, *she* always says she doesn't have money, but she does." Ashley referred to her mother. She squeezed herself down onto the sofa in the space where my head had been, where she could get a clear view of Richard in the dining room. "What happened to your glasses?" And, without waiting for an answer, lowered her voice to a whisper. "Did *he* give you anything?"

"Which question would you like me to answer first?"

"Oh, sorry." She giggled. "The glasses." She pretended that our relationship was the same. Had it changed only for me? I knew I would never again ride to school with her, or share homework, or entertain her when some boy was not available. I would not be her sidekick.

"I broke them skating," I said.

"Yesterday? I didn't know you—"

"This morning," I said. "Richard and I went skating this morning." I looked her straight in the eyes. If I had not known her so well, I would not have seen the almost imperceptible change behind her eyes when I said "Richard" instead of "Rich." Richard and I. It was so small, that alteration, it could not be called a change of expression—just a tiny light of recognition, of suspicion maybe.

119

"Did you do it on purpose? You look terrific." Her voice was low, conspiratorial.

Too ridiculous to answer.

"Bummer," she said. "Did he give you anything?"

I held up the book. "Dylan Thomas," I said.

"Oh, a book." I could tell that this was not something she would have wanted from him, and that she was delighted that I had received it. She didn't open it. Was I disappointed?

"Did you give him anything?"

"A book on the Boundary Waters."

She feigned disappointment in me. "You should have let me go with you to shop."

Suddenly, bad marriages came into clearer focus. I had had a bad marriage with Ashley, I realized, in a metaphorical sort of way. And now I wanted to throw a blender at her sexy little head.

"Oh, here's your present." She took a carefully wrapped package out of her canvas bag. "Merry Christmas," she said, leaning her cheek briefly against mine.

"Thanks," I said. "Yours is the green one under the tree."

I unwrapped a pair of black leather gloves, which I needed badly. "Thanks," I said. I didn't want them from her.

"They're for your dressy coat. Oh, it's just what I wanted," she shrieked, grasping the bright-colored Swatch I had given her.

"I know. You told me." I wished I'd bought something cheaper and then felt guilty. Where was my Christmas spirit?

She stood up to show it to Richard and Dad. "Isn't it great?" She stood behind Richard. "Look." She held it in front of his eyes, her head hovering near his, their cheeks almost touching. Why was I looking? I put my glasses in my lap.

"Oh, I brought you something," Ashley said.

It caught Richard off guard. "For me?"

"It's not very much," she cooed.

"Well, geez, uh—" His stammering made me smile.

"It's Obsession," she said. "If the fragrance fits—" He couldn't have finished unwrapping it yet. "It draws women like flies."

"Sounds like a burden," Dad muttered.

"Here, let me put some on you," Ashley said. I was glad I was blind.

"Uh, thanks, but I don't want to mix fragrances, as they say. Geez, that's really nice, Ash. Thanks." *The Romance Writer's Phrase Book* would say that Richard's voice was full of "disquiet."

"You can wear it on New Year's Eve—you're still planning to go, aren't you?"

More of that disquiet stuff: "Uh, yeah, sure. Looking forward to it."

Better get a tetanus shot.

The phone had rung and Mother had picked it up in the kitchen. "Your grandparents have arrived, Ashley. Your mother wants you to come home for dinner now."

"Okay, well—Merry Christmas, you guys."

I got up off the couch, my glasses in front of my face. "Thanks, Ash. Merry Christmas. Say hi to your mom." I walked her to the door.

121

"You're not wearing lip gloss, are you?" she said from the porch.

"No."

"You really should."

"Bye."

From the front hall, I looked at Richard through my pince-nez. "Don't like mixing fragrances, huh?" I laughed all the way back to the sofa.

"She was going to maul me to death. You saw her, Nels; she was going to maul me, wasn't she?" Richard pressed my dad.

"So what's your point?" Dad looked over his reading glasses at him.

Fleur and Mother came in from the kitchen. Seeing the wrappings on the table, Mother asked, "Who got the present?"

Richard held up the bottle of Obsession. "She wants me to wear it New Year's Eve."

"Sounds like the fattening before the kill," Fleur said.

Mother opened the bottle and sniffed. "Nels, why don't you get some of this—it's heavenly."

Richard grinned. "Like flies, Nels, like flies."

Dad patted his own cheek. "Maul me a little with that stuff, will you?" he said to Mother.

Fleur watched the two of them as if they were something special.

When Trish and Bjorn came back, we ate dinner: clam chowder and the leftovers from the night before. Then long-distance phone calls were made to my grandparents in Florida and my grandmother Bjorkman in Phoenix. Trish called her parents in Seattle, and Richard called his parents in Palo Alto. When he was finished, Mother talked to his mother, Caroline, for about forty-five minutes with the kitchen door closed. It was a combination of low whispers and loud shrieks of laughter. Heaven only knows what middle-aged women find interesting.

Fleur didn't call anyone.

By late afternoon, a quiet yearning was building in me: I wanted to be alone with Richard. It wasn't enough to share looks with him across the table when we all played Trivial Pursuit, girls against guys. (The girls won because Trish knew every single entertainment question, which was the biggest weakness with the rest of us.) Nor was it enough to play Scrabble with him in the window seat, our knees occasionally bumping at the side of the board. (I won by putting down all seven letters with "zymurgy." He took about half an hour taking his next turn, trying to match the points, while I repeated, "I've won, Bradshaw; give it up!") It wasn't enough to sit in front of the sofa on the floor with him, connected at the hip, so to speak, gazing into the fire. Dad dozed in his chair, occasionally making snarking noises that made us laugh. Trish, Fleur, and Mother worked on one of those puzzles with fifty million pieces. Bjorn, sprawled on the carpet in front of our feet, wanted to know where in the world Richard would live if money were no object.

"Here," Richard said.

"St. Paul?"

"Sure, why not?"

"St. Paul over Paris? Over Rome? Over London?"

"St. Paul is home," Richard said. "Besides, if you had

that much money, you could go anywhere you wanted anytime you wanted, so what does it matter where you live?"

"Yeah, but St. Paul—it's so provincial."

"It's home. Besides, I don't think it's so provincial. Provincial compared to what?"

Go to bed, I wanted to say. It's over. Christmas day is over. Now the day is over. How did that hymn go? Anyway, it is over. A fait accompli. Nighty-night. Goodnight Moon. The end. God bless us every one. Merry Christmas to all and to all a good night. Fini.

I yawned. Like magic, my dad awoke and said, "Let's call it a day, Becca. That puzzle won't get done in one night."

"I like the way Dad wakes up so he can go to bed," Bjorn said, standing up. He leaned over Trish at the table. "Honey?"

She patted his hand, which was on her shoulder, and fit one last piece onto the outer edge of the puzzle. "There, the border is almost done." She stood up. "Good night and thanks for a wonderful day." She kissed Mother's cheek.

It was like a choreographed dance. I had yawned and they had all gone into motion, except Richard, who stayed by my side in front of the sofa.

"I didn't realize it was so late already." Fleur looked at her watch. "It was a wonderful day. Merry Christmas."

They shuffled in clusters into the front hall. Mother looked back at me briefly, her mouth open as if she wanted to say something, give advice maybe, but happily she thought better of it. "Good night, Kate, Rich.

Merry Christmas." She gave us one of those funny looks of hers that I wouldn't want to analyze.

And then they were gone. All of them.

Richard pulled my arm through his and held on to my hand. "I thought they'd never leave," he said. "I thought I would grow old in this room with all of them watching."

I leaned my head against him. "A conspiracy," I said.

He smiled, kissing my hair, my mouth. "This may be the best Christmas day yet," he murmured.

"Sure beats Ruffy's doo-doo."

He laughed. We were changing positions to something I liked better. I was solidly in his arms now, pressed against him. *The Romance Writer's Phrase Book* has lots of hot descriptions for that "pressing against" position, but it just doesn't sound like me—like something I'd say.

We kissed. He smelled of soap. We kissed. The clock in the front hall ticked. We kissed. We kissed paragraphs' worth. I'm so dizzy remembering it, I can hardly concentrate on writing it down.

Once when we came up for air, he said, "I don't want to go to that party with Ashley. Can't you and I arrange—"

I shook my head. "I asked Helmut weeks ago. I think he's even bought a suit."

"Are you and he—you know?"

"We're debate partners!"

He smiled. "That's it?"

"You want there to be more?"

"I mean—"

"He's an exchange student from Berlin. I wanted to practice my German. That's how we got to be friends. Last year I didn't take a date and my aunt has been threatening all year to fix me up with someone. I asked Helmut in self-defense."

Richard's mouth moved along my throat. "I hate the guy already."

"No, he's nice. He'll probably want to ask you about Stanford."

"I'm cutting in on all the slow dances—every damned one."

"Mmm. Ashley won't like that."

"A whole night with her—the longest night of the year." He groaned. "She's so nuts."

I couldn't disagree with that. "We can dance in the kitchen after it's over."

Pages of kissing. Literally pages. You'd be bored. I had moved up the hierarchy of those who are happy at Christmas. I had moved into the top slot. I was in love and I was pretty sure that Richard was in love with me, although he hadn't said as much yet. But actions speak louder than words, unless the guy is out of one of those summer beach movies filled with oversexed sociopaths. I knew Richard was better than that. I trusted him completely.

Revision Notes

My parents sound too perfect. All that good humor, all that affection, not to mention the good cooking, will make readers want to puke, or will make them think their own parents are horrific duds. My parents are okay, but I've made them depressingly good-natured. Somehow I need to work in their weaknesses. Here's a list of ten items each:

My Father's Weaknesses and Imperfections:

1. He has never in his life attended any PTA meeting or school function that I or Bjorn has participated in. Never. "Your mother will make a video," he says.
2. He has never watched one of Mother's videos.
3. He thinks the Boy Scouts of America is a fascist organization and that Eagle Scouts grow up to become serial killers. He did allow Bjorn to join the Scout troop, but he made him promise not to make Eagle.
4. He farts whenever and wherever he pleases.
5. When driving, he weaves across lanes and breaks for green lights, and if anyone complains, he'll stop the car in the middle of traffic.
6. He has a little paunch and moles all over his back.
7. If Mother didn't choose his clothes, he'd wear black dress shoes and black socks with his jeans.

A couple of alcoholic rages might improve this list, but I'd be lying. Oh, he does go into a rage if anyone removes the stapler or paper punch from his study and doesn't return it. That could be number 8.

9. I can't think of anything else.
10. Still can't think.

My Mother's Weaknesses and Imperfections:

1. This first one is easy. Even my dad doesn't know. Occasionally she goes down to the basement to have a smoke. I've known this since I was five. Marlboro Lights. Not often, just occasionally. So she's a hypocrite.
2. Of the good, the true, and the beautiful, she ranks beauty first without hesitation. (Which is why she has no problem with a little hypocrisy.)
3. She hates cats. Especially cat motifs in decorating—like needlepoint cats, cat calendars. Even kittens. Thinks they should be crushed like cockroaches. (Guess I won't put that in the book.)
4. She thinks long-stemmed roses are a cliché. But is that really a weakness?
5. She enjoys dirty jokes. Jokes too filthy to tell in this book.
6. When anyone asks her if either of her children is as gifted visually as she is, she replies, "No, they take after Nels—they're both visual pygmies."
7. She adores gossip.
8. She can't resist looking at herself in any mirror or plate-glass window.

9. When she's burned out after a big job, she won't talk.
10. If it weren't for Nair, she'd have a little mustache. (If she ever reads this, she'll kill me.)

Pretty lame lists. They lack violence. I could tell about the famous fight. The one that has become family folklore. This is the way Mother tells it:

Oh, that fight! It was years ago, of course. Nels and I were both young and hormonal. He said something hurtful to me. I honestly don't remember what it was. Don't have a clue. I got angry and raged through the house, slamming doors and kicking things.

Nels felt terrible immediately and began following after me and saying how he wished he'd never said it, whatever it was, and, please, would I forgive him. I didn't want to forgive him. I wanted him dead, preferably torn apart by ravenous rottweilers. But he wouldn't just let me go and cool off. He wanted to fix it right then. Nels gets kind of pathetic and cloying when I'm mad at him.

Anyway, I locked myself upstairs in the master bathroom, filled the tub with water, removed my clothes, and got in. Nels stood on the other side of the door and begged me to let him in. I told him to drop dead. Then he began to take the doorknob and lock apart. I was shouting, "Get out of here. Can't you leave me alone?" Really, I was crazy.

He brought in the desk chair, the one with the cotton uphol-stered seat, and before he could sit down on it, I took a washrag filled with water and slapped it down onto that seat.

He looked at the seat. He looked at me. I could see the

wheels turning in his head. And then he stepped into the tub and sat down—with all his clothes on and he was wearing wool tweed! He was even wearing his shoes! We were both crammed into that tub.

What could I do except burst out laughing. And then I cried and told him he had hurt my feelings and let him tell me he was sorry. And we made up.

When Mother tells this story, Dad always says, "Yes, we did," with the kind of smirk you don't like to see on a parent's face. Who wants to think about their parents doing it? All that flab meshed together. Disgusting. And I'm trying to point out their weaknesses, but they tell this story themselves, dramatizing the details and making fun of themselves. Mother says, "I was being very neurotic."

The story may be too charming to tell. I told it to Shannon, and she thought it was a very romantic thing for my father to do. She practically swooned at the idea, even though he's an old man. And that's exactly what I don't want to do, tell yet another story that makes them look charming. I'm going to have to think about this some more.

This chapter, Chapter Ten, a short chapter, has nothing to do with romance or kissing or pressing breasts against corded muscles. Nothing at all. But I feel compelled, as Midgely used to say, to tell you. I have been surprised as I write this how often Midgely is mentioned on these pages. How often I quote him. I have made him a minor character in this novel without meaning to. His influence has altered who I am in nearly imperceptible ways. I'm barely recognizing it now.

He had legs like tree trunks before the cancer. He didn't look like a tennis player at all—too large, too squarely built, more like a wrestler or a tackle. For that matter, he didn't look much like an English teacher either. Not dapper and sensitive like Mr. Harcourt, or sardonic like Mr. Voight, or owly like Ms. Janacek. He was red-faced and freckled, and he had been losing his strawberry-blond hair even before the chemotherapy.

It snowed all Christmas night, and when I awoke, a Jeep and a Blazer were stuck in the middle of our street, stuck in what must have been more than three feet of snow. I saw it through pince-nez.

Mary Lou Midgely stepped from her front porch, her parka unzipped, and plowed laboriously through the snow to the Blazer to talk with its driver.

Dad and Bjorn, without coats, made their way from the house to the Blazer as well, for what now looked like a conference.

Something was up. I met Mother in the hallway. "Midge needs to go to the hospital," she said, placing folded towels in the linen closet, "but nothing can get through—no ambulance, no four-wheel-drive vehicles —nothing."

"What about snowplows?"

"We've called. They're all on main thoroughfares. The city's got a crisis on its hands. This is a record snowfall for one night. Better get dressed," she said.

But I'm so happy today, I thought, brushing my teeth. Midgely can't go to the hospital today, the day after Christmas, today, when I'm happy. Today when I'm in love and beloved. This is too joyous a day for anyone to be going to the hospital. Time is wrapped in red-and-green taffeta ribbon today.

I knew better, of course. It was Midgely, after all, who taught me about logical fallacies last year. Why is it that logic hardly ever makes emotional sense?

It was an hour and a half later that a plow, one of those gigantic yellow cats that can plow half a street at a time, drove through our neighborhood looking like a resurrected dinosaur. An ambulance followed it. I'm sure everyone in our house was standing by a window somewhere.

I stood in front of the living room window, gazing through pince-nez across the white slope of the lawn, across the white street to Midgely's house, where the front door was opening. Richard stood behind me, his hands on my shoulders.

The ambulance drivers, probably realizing that a gurney was useless in the snow, carried Midgely out on a white stretcher covered in white blankets. They moved cautiously but quickly down the front walk of Midgely's house and, reaching the sidewalk, turned toward the ambulance, which did not stand directly in front of the house but was parked at the corner. It was not until they turned that I saw Midgely's face, yellow as tennis balls against the new snow. Yellow and contorted and unrecognizable.

I think I held my breath until he was in the ambulance, until Mary Lou was in the ambulance with him, until the ambulance followed the giant yellow cat out of our neighborhood. I was left with the white snow, the blue winter sky, and Richard's warm hands on my shoulders.

None of it made any sense at all.

Sometimes novelists find it necessary to get rid of a character to further the plot. I mean *David Copperfield* would hardly be the bildungsroman it is if Dickens hadn't killed off David's mother, leaving David in care of the wicked Mr. Murdstone and his equally wicked sister, Miss Murdstone. It's then that all David's problems begin, and they continue for eight hundred pages or so until the resolution.

In this, *my* story, there have been relatively few problems. Ashley has been a pain, but nothing I couldn't handle. Richard loves me; that's been well established. Things are running too smoothly. You're probably getting bored. So I'm going to zap Fleur in Chapter Eleven, because if she stays in the novel any longer, there will be no unhappiness on New Year's Eve, and that's what this story needs: a little unhappiness, a little contrast, so that you'll appreciate the happy resolution. Trust me on this.

As a novelist, I have many choices when it comes to zapping Fleur. I could have her struck by a minibus while crossing Nicollet Avenue in downtown Minneapolis. The doughnuts, iced with chocolate frosting, she had just bought would be strewn in the street, the angora scarf I gave her still wrapped around her lovely throat. A scene full of pathos and anguish. You'd probably cry.

Or I could have her commit suicide because of the humiliation of having her mother marry for the sixth time. I, the protagonist, would find her hanging from the light fixture in my bedroom, her face gray and distorted. I'd cut her down and give her mouth-to-mouth resuscitation for half an hour to no avail.

Not very plausible for a survivor like Fleur or for a happy genre like the romance novel either. I'll tell you what *really* happened. She left to see her mother marry, but not before she took me to the ophthalmologist's and helped me with my Desdemona paper.

Fleur. Flower. Not a fragile one either. A sunflower, maybe, or a zinnia. A flower full of piss and vinegar. "Fleur isn't my real name—it's Diane. I got Fleur when I was eight and in the habit of stealing flowers in the neighborhood for drying. You know, you hang them upside down and they dry with the petals still open. I had them in baskets and vases and jelly jars—dried flowers all over the house. That's when my father named me Fleur, and it stuck."

It's the day after Christmas when she's telling me this. We were seated in the Cherokee, Fleur driving, me in the passenger seat, my pince-nez taped with masking tape to my nose and forehead. My whole head shouted "nerd alert!" But I was tired of holding them. "Fleur fits you better than Diane," I said. "Thievery fits you too, some-how."

She smiled. "Yes, a flower thief, but of course I stole only to preserve them."

"Robin Hood of the flowers," I said. "Sounds very noble. Turn right at the light." We were headed for the ophthalmologist's office across from Rosedale. "Was that in Newport Beach? Your life of crime?" I was aware again of the way she sometimes dropped her postvocalic "r's."

"No, we moved there when I was thirteen; before that we were in—"

"Let me guess!" I shouted it. "Oh, sorry, we were sup-posed to turn left back there."

"I'll turn at the corner," she said. "Go ahead, guess. Your dad guessed this morning. Got it right on the first try."

We followed a snowplow into the parking lot. "He's better than I am," I said, "but it's East Coast and it's south of Baltimore. Right?"

She nodded. She was wearing the angora muffler I had given her loosely about her head, and she looked gorgeous. "Very good," she said.

"But it's not as far south as Savannah—don't tell me!"

She laughed. "This close enough?" She pulled into a parking place.

"As a matter of fact," I continued, "I don't think it's south of North Carolina—"

"Your dad didn't need this much speculating." She turned off the ignition. "Take your best shot, Kate."

"Raleigh, North Carolina, or maybe Winston-

136

Salem—no, I'll go with Raleigh." I pushed the pince-nez and tape against the bridge of my nose and stared at her face. "Yes?"

"Yes. It's Raleigh." She laughed when I made two victorious fists. "Your dad said it was the diphthongs that gave me away."

"Don't tell him how long it took me," I said, getting out of the Cherokee.

Fleur sat in the corner of Dr. Carver's examining room while I had my eyes checked. "You know," Dr. Carver said, rolling his stool back, "you might try the contact lenses again—see if you've outgrown that intolerance. Most kids do at some point, and contacts are a lot better now than they were even a few years ago. How long has it been since you tried contacts?"

"Three years," I said.

"It'd be nice not to have to wear these Coke bottles anymore, wouldn't it?" He tapped my knee with his ballpoint pen.

I retaped the pince-nez to my face. "I don't know—I think I look pretty glamorous this way, don't you?" I twisted my head to an odd angle and looked at him cross-eyed.

But inside, the thought of contact lenses made my stomach churn. The timing seemed all wrong. Richard, my hero, fell in love with me wearing the glasses. It seemed so romance-novel-like to appear suddenly without them, transformed from the geeky-looking schoolgirl into the standard romantic heroine, except taller. It should have been exactly the opposite, but taking the glasses *off* felt more phony than keeping them. It

137

felt like putting on lip gloss. Ashley would approve fully. Maybe that's why it all seemed contrived. I didn't, I realized, even want to be the standard romantic heroine. I didn't want to be transformed, and especially not for New Year's Eve. It all seemed too calculated, even though I hadn't planned it that way.

"You want to try them? They could be ready in a couple of days." Dr. Carver nudged me out of my reflection.

I looked at Fleur, who slouched in her chair, her fingers laced lightly together across her abdomen. Her face showed no opinion.

"I don't think I want to—not now. I mean—that is—" Geez, I sounded so stupid. What could I say? I don't want to be transformed into a raving beauty? As if I even had a chance of that. "I—I'm just not ready." I was stammering. "Maybe in a couple of months."

Was that why Fleur smiled ever so slightly, because I was stammering? Damn her.

Back in the Cherokee, driving to the university library, she said, "The idea of wearing contact lenses embarrassed you. You blushed."

There's no point in arguing with Fleur when she's already guessed the truth. No point at all. "It felt too much like a transformation," I said. "I'm having this romance with Richard at Christmastime and then suddenly I get a chance to look like a real human girl—"

"A rather pretty girl, at that." Fleur watched the road.

"It felt like tempting fate—too much of a good thing. Too romantic for words." I cupped my hands on either side of my glasses as if to keep them lodged against my face for safety.

"Your whole life has been a romance," Fleur said, gripping the steering wheel more tightly. "Your parents, your house, your neighborhood, your schooling, your brother, your friends, your tennis lessons, your German lessons, your linguistics lessons, your traditional Swedish Christmas with all the trimmings—everything, even with the cataracts, even if you never loved Rich or he you, your whole life would still be a romance. I feel like the Little Match Girl looking in."

That's what Fleur St. Germaine, the most beautiful, the smartest, the most independent, the everything-I-wanted-to-be girl said to me the day after Christmas. She had given me the briefest of looks. Fleur as the Little Match Girl? I didn't know what to say.

At the university library, reading about Desdemona again depressed Fleur. She dropped her forehead onto the wooden table with a mild thud. Her blond hair hid her face. "Totally depressing," she said.

I thought she meant the ending of the play, when Othello strangles Desdemona.

"She reminds me of my mother." Her voice was garbled behind her hair.

I laid my head down on my arms next to her. "Who?"

"Desdemona. Desdemona reminds me of my mother." She turned her head so that her cheek lay flat on the table. "My mother sees her future husbands' 'visage' in her mind. She consecrates herself to them. All of them. And in the end all of her husbands strangle her—metaphorically speaking, of course."

"Even your dad?"

"Twice."

"Twice?"

"He told her the first time they were married that monogamy was not for him and then went on to prove it to her many times."

He sounded much like Ashley's father.

"He was also husband number three, because although he had an aversion to monogamy, he was charming and handsome and all of those romantic qualities that my mother falls for and that match her hats." Fleur blew her hair from her eyes. "He looked like that old movie star Tyrone Power. Do you know him?"

"A guy with a mustache?"

"No." She snickered. "My mother doesn't like facial hair."

"What about the second husband?" I said, whispering because a girl with a huge stack of books had sat down at the end of our table.

"A Vietnam veteran. Purple Heart. Big and brave. Just like Othello. Nice too, except when he was drunk. He was drunk a lot."

"And number four?"

"An old guy, Foster. Don't know much about him." She lifted her head slightly and smirked. "He died of a heart attack on their wedding night."

"You're making it up."

"I wish."

"Number five?"

"Had ties to the Mafia."

"You *are* making these up!"

"No."

"Number six?"

"Haven't met him. He's her plastic surgeon. She says she's found happiness at last."

"Maybe it's true this time." I didn't really believe it.

"About as true as those TV miniseries that my mother seems to be copying. Life copying TV." She sat up. "I'm whining," she said.

"It's refreshing to find you have a weakness," I said. "Come on. I've got all the articles I need. Let's go home."

Driving through our neighborhood, looking at the bare branches of elms arching over the streets, heavy with snow, at the windows lit with yellow lights, at the streetlamps glowing softly, I began to see that my life *was* a romance. And as we pulled into the garage, I realized that I had always expected my parents to be there, together, pleasant, humorous, understanding, and they were.

Later that evening at the airport, when Fleur's flight had been called for boarding, she said to us, "Rich told me there was a splendid neighborhood in St. Paul where George Bailey and his family still lived. I thought he was lying his head off, but I believe him now." She looked fondly at my parents.

"I do have a striking resemblance to the young Jimmy Stewart," Dad said.

Bjorn snorted. "In your dreams, old man."

"Pleeze," my mother said. "I'm no Mary Bailey. I always thought Donna Reed was smarmy—all that patient smiling."

"But you're not Joan Collins either." Fleur laughed. "I'll try the recipes."

"Call me," Mother said and hugged her hard. "You have the number."

"Memorized," Fleur said. "Good-bye, handsome." She pecked my dad's lips and hugged him.

"Come back." He kissed her hand. "Chocolates are waiting in the kitchen cupboard."

She hugged Bjorn and Trish. "Next year, let *her* pick the tree!" she teased Bjorn. Then she hugged Richard. "I owe you," she said. "Thanks for letting me come."

He nodded.

I pulled a red recorder out of my parka. "Here," I said, handing it to Fleur. "Something to remember us by."

"My own recorder!" She grasped it tightly.

"Next time we'll play a trio," I said. "Or you can find someone else to play with."

"Maybe someday."

We held on to each other. "You're not your mother, Fleur. You're not Desdemona either."

Still holding on to me, she moved her head away from my face and looked at me, grinning. "And you'll still be the Kate Bjorkman we all know and love even without those glasses." We laughed at each other then, like girls, hysterical, fluttery, romantic, pleased with our closing speeches.

"Oh, here," I said, digging into my pockets. "Some Polaroids to remember us by."

"I'll have more pictures when I can get back to my darkroom," Trish said.

The Polaroids put me on the verge of crying, but the final boarding call saved me from myself. Fleur, with carry-on luggage, recipes, her own recorder, and photographs, blew kisses and walked down the jetway. Exit Fleur St. Germaine.

There's this old idea that fiction writing should imitate real life, that the situations and the characters must seem plausible to the reader. The trouble I'm having with beginning this chapter, Chapter Twelve, has to do with that idea. See, the problem is that sometimes life is a whole lot more absurd than any imagination can conjure up. Like last year Maren Jacobson wrote this short story for Midgely's unit on creative writing. In this story, a woman drops fifty floors at high speed in a broken elevator. Not only does the woman survive, but she steps out of the elevator and asks, "Have I passed the mezzanine?"

When Maren read this aloud to the class, we all just about passed out. "Give us a break," we said.

Midgely held up his hand—"Wait"—and, turning to Maren, said, "The class, understandably I think, is having trouble accepting this scene." The corners of his mouth twitched up slightly, but his voice was kind. "It sounds pretty far-fetched, don't you think? Especially since the rest of the story is so realistic."

Maren, who grasped the pages of her story as if she might fall into a hole, said, "But it really happened!"

"Be serious," we said.

"It did! My aunt LaPriel—"

That cracked us up—that name, LaPriel. It sounded like a picante sauce.

Midgely quieted us with his raised hand. He could do that, but he was the only one who could. "Go on," he told Maren.

"Aunt LaPriel fell fifty stories in an elevator in the Chrysler Building in New York City in 1947. She worked there as a mail clerk and later married and had three children. It's true!"

"We believe you," Midgely said. "But the question is does this 'true story' work in the fiction?"

Midgely's question is loud in my ear right now, even though he's lying in the hospital with a thousand tubes in him. It's his voice that has kept me from saying more about New Year's Eve. It's like Maren's aunt LaPriel—real life—but you're not going to buy it. I'm just going to have to ask you to do as Coleridge said: suspend your disbelief.

Here goes: I have a rich aunt, my father's sister, who lives in a pink stucco mansion way out on Lake Minnetonka—a house she bought completely furnished after it was showcased one spring for charity. Every year she throws this enormous dinner-dance on New Year's Eve, and her name is Eve. Get it? New Year's *Eve*. It is so incredibly stupid, but the thing is, it's true. I'm not making this up. But why am I being defensive? This book is not even fiction really; it's my life. Think of it more as autobiography. I mean if this were fiction, would I make up a name like Eve for a woman whose whole identity comes from throwing an annual New Year's Eve party? Would I make up New Year's *Eve?* Never. I swear it on that Dylan Thomas book with Richard's inscription in the front.

Anyway, Aunt Eve married Uncle Lanny, whose family got stinking rich in the grain business a couple of generations ago, which is why we call him the Doughboy. That and because he looks like the Pillsbury Doughboy: cherubic and pale. He also speaks with a high voice and giggles a lot.

When I say "we" call Uncle Lanny "Doughboy," I mean Bjorn and me. Dad calls Lanny the "White Eunuch"—behind his back at least. (Lanny and Eve never had children.) Dad's usually not that acerbic, but Lanny is always taking tacky digs at him, like "I guess a schoolteacher's salary doesn't go very far these days," or "Becca's probably making more than you with that designing business of hers, huh?"

So my dad, who loves to dance with my mother, despises this party. Usually his narcolepsy kicks in for the entire New Year's Eve day and my mother has to wake him to get showered and wake him again to get dressed. Sometimes she has to drive him there herself. "Eve would be so insulted if her little brother didn't show up for this one party," she tells him when he rebels.

But this year there was no sign of rebellion. "I'm resigned," he said at lunch. "The White Eunuch has won."

Raised eyebrows all around.

It was Richard who lay like a dead slug on the sofa, eyes rolled toward the ceiling. "Tell Ashley," he said as I swung past on the way to Dad's study, "that I have the mumps. Mumps are dangerous in a grown man."

"Could turn *you* into a white eunuch." I laughed and pulled my paper on Desdemona from the printer tray.

"Might be preferable," Richard muttered.

"You don't have to marry her; it's just one night," I said, whisking past him again.

He caught my arm and pulled me down onto the sofa. "What are you doing walking back and forth so efficiently?"

"Don't crinkle my Desdemona paper," I said, holding it up.

"Is that what you've been working on all morning?"

I nodded. "I just have to pull my Works Cited page together and I'm finished."

"Stay here a minute." He raised my hand to his lips. *"Ich küsse die Hand."* He kissed my hand. "That's what that *GQ* god from Berlin will be saying to you, no doubt."

I laughed hard then. "Maybe he'll say, '*Ich küsse die Lippen.*'" I kissed him lightly on his *Lippen.*

"Hell."

"Richard." I laughed. "I've never seen you so—so—"

"Inadequate? Petty? Whiny? Boring? Stop me when I come to it. Feeble? Lame?"

"Stop." I couldn't stop laughing.

"Imperfect, deficient, sour—"

"Wow, only Mr. Radio could come up with a string ⌐f adjectives like that."

He smiled. "That blabbermouth, Fleur."

147

"She said you were a smoothie."

"What does she know?" He pulled me down and kissed me, one of those breast-on-chest kisses that I refuse to describe further to you. Faces pleasantly mashed into each other. Arms gripping. All that stuff.

"Kate, I don't want to go with Ashley at all, in case you haven't noticed. She could look like Miss Universe and I'd still feel deprived, because I want to spend New Year's Eve with you, and I want you with me and not horny Helmut."

He was too funny. "Helmut is so harmless," I said. The thought of Helmut as horny made me giggle uncontrollably.

"Well," he said, "Ashley isn't harmless." There was a glint in his eye. "I'll have to carry a baseball bat, or a raygun. I'll have to wear a raincoat and a Plexiglas mask!"

I burst out in fresh laughter.

"Maybe a suit of armor," Richard continued. "I've got it—skunk oil!"

"Will you cut it out?"

He grinned. "How did she get invited to your aunt's party anyway?"

"Same way you always got invited—friend of the family."

He growled.

"Aunt Eve sends Ashley her own invitation now, and she'll continue to until I ask her to stop." Which I would do this year.

"Let's meet after the dance, here, at one." He patted the sofa.

"That's too early," I said. "It takes forty minutes to get back, maybe more if it starts snowing again."

"Two?"

"Yes, two, here. If we're late—"

"Oh please, let's not be later than two." He groaned again. "I'll be here at two."

"Same here."

Kiss kiss. Embrace embrace. Sigh sigh. Et cetera et cetera.

THAT EVENING WHEN I stepped into the hall wearing my new glasses and looking as great as I knew how to look in black velvet with gold rope trim on the bodice, I met Richard coming out of his room looking stunning in a tuxedo. My stomach curled, and I was immediately sorry that I had not phoned Helmut to call the night off. Sorry that we had not told Ashley to stuff it, politely, of course. "You look beautiful," I said. "Edible, in fact."

"You're stealing my lines, I think."

We stood eyeballing each other.

He stepped forward. "We could still call Ashley and Helmut—"

"Helmut's downstairs," I said. "Come and meet him."

Richard made a noise deep in his throat that sounded like "arrgh." He leaned forward and kissed me lightly. "This night is one grand charade," he said.

"Is that Obsession I smell?"

He colored slightly. "Appealing?"

"Very." We moved down the stairs together. "I thought you were going to wear scent of skunk oil."

149

"I'm afraid it would turn her on."

I laughed. He was so handsome, it made me dizzy walking down the stairs next to him, and I have to confess that I was filled with yearning and longing and all those euphemisms for sexual desire. "His closeness was like a drug, lulling her to euphoria." That's what the phrase book might say.

I was hot for Richard but going out with Helmut, alas, who waited for me in the front room looking quite Teutonic in a dark suit. Quite handsome, really. I was grateful to have him look so good in front of Richard—grateful that his cowlick was flattened down for once. I introduced them to each other and they shook hands. "Richard is our houseguest," I explained. "He grew up down the block. He's a friend of Bjorn's. He's at Stanford." Ta duh, ta duh, ta duh.

They muttered greetings at each other. Helmut was stiff and formal, a little nervous. I felt sorry for him. Richard was completely relaxed, if not downright smug.

Mother appeared looking radiant in a pale-pink gown and insisted on taking our picture with a Polaroid camera. "Stand by the fireplace," she said to Helmut and me.

"Mother," I objected.

"It w"   less." She smiled pleasantly, one of those phony smiles parents use when they're not going to pay any attention to your requests. "A little closer together," she said, looking through the camera lens.

"Mother!"

Helmut clutched my waist, and I realized that he too was wearing Obsession. This fact, and Richard smirking behind Mother's shoulder, made me want to laugh. In fact, an uncontrollable nervous giggle may have emerged as Mother pushed the button and we were blinded by the flash.

"Now take one of Kate and me." A glint of humor crossed Richard's face. He stepped between Helmut and me. "Excuse me," he said, smiling benignly at Helmut, who looked bewildered.

So did Mother, but she collected herself quickly. "Will you hold this?" She handed the snapshot to Helmut. "I think it's going to be a good one."

"This one will be a good one too," Richard said, an easy smile on his lips. One arm was around my shoulder. "Smile pretty," he said to me. He deserved to be punched.

Another flash.

"Now take one of the three of us," Richard said devilishly (that's how the phrase book describes that look). "Come on, Helmut." He stood between me and Helmut, an arm around each of us, pulling us toward him. "You kids smile now," he said. He was grinning foolishly at Mother, who was laughing softly behind the camera.

Flash.

"Now take one of Helmut and me," Richard said, removing his arm from my shoulder but keeping his arm around Helmut.

Even Helmut laughed then. "Your friend has a screw loose, no?" he said, his accent thick.

"A screw loose, yes. Come on, let's go." I pulled Helmut into the front hall, put on my coat, and whisked him out the front door.

"You kids have a good time!" Richard called.

Even with the front door shut, I could hear him and Mother laughing.

Believe it or not, Helmut and I debated the Whorfian hypothesis all the way to Minnetonka. It's a hypothesis I don't really buy. I mean I just don't think that language determines ideas and perceptions any more than clothes determine your body type, but Helmut in his sweet anal-retentive way argued that the German word *Staubsauger*—dust sucker—reflects a more functional way of seeing than the English equivalent, "vacuum cleaner." As we drove down the curved driveway of the Pink Palace, glittering like the starship *Enterprise* in the crisp winter night, he said to me, "You are the only one I can discuss linguistics with."

I suppose for Helmut it was a kind of declaration of love. His intentions were good, but I couldn't help comparing him to Richard, who would have guffawed at the idea of romancing a girl with the Whorfian hypothesis.

There were already a lot of people gathered in the "front salon," as Uncle Lanny calls it, a phrase that makes my father's eyes roll to the back of his head. After we had given our coats to a man hired to take our coats, we met Aunt Eve and Uncle Lanny, who had organized themselves into kind of a two-person receiving line. Eve hugged me hard. "If I didn't have this party, I'd never see my favorite niece," she said.

"Oh come on," I said. "I'm here all summer long."

"Is this one special?" she whispered loudly in my ear.

"Aunt Eve!" I protested.

Uncle Lanny questioned Helmut about the "united

Berlin" but didn't listen to any of the answers. Instead he blustered, "This is *the* party in the Twin Cities. Hubert Humphrey used to come to this party, you know."

I saw the puzzlement behind Helmut's polite smile. He had no idea who Hubert Humphrey was.

Uncle Lanny winked at me. "Isn't that right, Katie, my girl?"

"That's what I've heard," I said. Uncle Lanny had always been kind to me, but I knew Dad was right. He *was* an old gasbag.

Helmut and I wandered from room to room, each decorated with great glittering trees and wreaths in all the tall, elegant windows, which in daylight gave a view of Lake Minnetonka.

Helmut gaped a great deal. "What does your uncle do for a living?" he asked finally.

"He goes to his office every day and watches his portfolio."

He looked puzzled.

"His investments," I said.

"He doesn't work, then?"

I laughed. "He takes care of his money. He's good at it too, from what I've heard." I led him into the dining room, where an elaborate buffet was laid out. The room was lit with candlelight only. People were lined up on each side of a long table. Helmut and I stood in line. Across the room I saw Trish and Bjorn talking to one of Bjorn's old classmates. I waved to Trish, who made her way over to us.

"I'm Trish Bjorkman," she said to Helmut before I

could introduce them. "You must be Helmut." They shook hands.

She lowered her voice. "Have you seen your friend Ashley?"

I shook my head.

"She is making them faint in the next room."

"What do you mean?"

"She's—" She stopped, her attention focused beyond my shoulder.

I turned my head and saw Ashley in the doorway. I may have stopped breathing. She was definitely not wearing the dress she had shown me at Christmas. Instead she was poured into a strapless black number with her breasts perched halfway out of the top. Her hair was thick and curled and swung around her shoulders. Her long, black-stockinged legs, perfectly shaped, showed from midthigh on down. She looked older, sophisticated—I would like to say that she looked cheap, but it wouldn't be true. She looked dramatic, like a model out of *Harper's Bazaar*. She looked sensuous as hell. She wore the diamond earrings and a necklace that matched. Dozens of heads turned to look, to appreciate, to be stunned.

Richard stood behind her, talking to Uncle Lanny, whose face was florid. Lanny couldn't take his eyes off Ashley, even if it was only her back he was seeing. Richard didn't look at Ashley at all. How much energy, I wondered, did it take to avoid those creamy shoulders, those creamy boobs, that perfect-looking face and figure?

My throat constricted the way it does when I'm afraid.

154

"Can you believe it?" Trish was whispering.

"Wow," I said, trying to keep my voice light, trying to push the panic down.

"Is that Ashley Cooper?" Helmut stared across the room.

"It's one version," I said, immediately regretting the bite in my voice, but Helmut seemed not to notice; his attention was focused completely on Ashley.

"Incredible, isn't it?" Trish said. "Watch out, she's gunning—" She turned. "Bjorn's looking for me. See you in a bit." She disappeared back into the crowd.

I spooned indiscriminately onto my plate. I knew who Ashley was gunning for. "Let's go sit in the other room," I said to Helmut.

He followed me like an obedient dog. We sat on a sofa. I talked about past-participle morphs in English in the most animated manner I could. And what is funny is that Helmut was actually interested in my textbook parroting. It was depressing. The food all tasted like bran flakes.

Mother and Dad came by on their way to the dining room. Dad leaned down and whispered, "You look lovely." There was such disparity between that statement and the way I actually felt, which was homely and lumpy—my new tortoiseshell glasses seemed three feet thick—that I wanted to bawl. I felt as if my whole life were at stake.

And then, as if I needed further reminder, Ashley and Richard walked into the room with plates of food. Obviously, Mother and Dad were seeing Ashley for the first time. Dad said, "Lord almighty," and Mother said, "Where on earth is that child's mother?"

From upstairs we could hear the orchestra starting up in the ballroom.

"Hi, you guys." Ashley sat down next to me. Richard sat in a chair across from us.

"You exchanged your dress," I said to Ashley.

She leaned into me. "I wanted something more *tantalizing*." Her words exactly.

"How did you get past your mother?" It was depressing how much I wanted to know.

"She went out much earlier with Doug. They were going to some steak house across the St. Croix in Wisconsin. Do you like it?" She meant the dress.

"You're creating quite a stir," I said. Heads were constantly turning in her direction.

Except for Richard's. He was speaking in low tones with Dell Bradshaw, the youngest Minneapolis city councilman and Richard's cousin.

Ashley leaned across me to say something to Helmut, who blushed uncontrollably whenever he had to look at her.

I gazed across Ashley's shoulder at Richard, who looked up at me and gave me "a smile as intimate as a kiss." The phrase book got that just right. It was a "slow, secret smile," a smile I understood perfectly. Richard loved *me*. Ashley could wear sequins and tassels— Richard loved me. *Moi*. That smile lifted me out of my despair. "Let's go dance," I said to Helmut, getting up.

"Save one for me," Ashley cooed to Helmut, who looked as if his head would explode.

Richard caught my hand as I passed him and pulled me down to whisper in my ear: "Remember, all the slow dances are mine."

I nodded. I have to confess that I "gloried briefly in the shared moment." But why shouldn't I glory?

Richard was true to his promise. The first half hour of dancing was filled with lively, fast music. Helmut was a better dancer than I would have supposed. The music seemed to relax him. But when the first slow song came up, Richard was there asking for an exchange. Ashley smiled cooperatively.

Richard pulled me close, his lips pressed against my forehead. "At last," he murmured. I felt completely reassured.

Ashley's expansive smile decreased with every slow-dance exchange. I didn't care. Richard sang an old Cole Porter tune in my ear: "Night and day, you are the one." Ashley could rage all she wanted. She had the attention. I had Richard.

The night continued that way, divided for me between fast dancing and slow dancing until about half an hour before midnight, when the orchestra played "Stardust"—definitely a slow one, but Richard and Ashley were nowhere in sight. I supposed Ashley had put her foot down.

"Aha, you will have to dance one slow dance with me," Helmut teased. He had not exactly suffered dancing them with Ashley. Over his shoulder I searched for Richard. He was not in the room.

A couple of fast dances and then another slow dance. Still no Richard. Hats and noisemakers, bags of confetti, and rolls of streamers were passed to all the guests. Just before midnight Uncle Lanny led the countdown, using an old European clock housed in a porcelain case to tell the "correct" time. The crowd, vibrating, more than a little drunk, counted backward together: "Ten, nine, eight, seven . . ." A drumroll accompanied them.

Where was Richard?

"Six, five, four . . ." I wanted Richard to begin this new year. "Three, two, one—" Happy New Year! The orchestra struck up "Auld Lang Syne." Helmut kissed me politely on the lips. "*Frohes Neujahr*," he said warmly.

"*Ein glückliches Neues Jahr, mein deutsches Freund.*" I hugged him, and then we made noise and threw streamers and confetti and shouted "Happy New Year" in German.

Where was Richard?

Outside, fireworks went up near the boat dock, and guests gravitated to the long windows to look out. When I was a child, this was my favorite part of the party. Helmut said the whole city of Berlin lit up with firecrackers at New Year's. "This makes me homesick," he said, his eyes cast upward. I was glad I had brought him.

Mother and Dad, Trish and Bjorn all came by to kiss me and wish me Happy New Year, and I thought of Fleur telling me my whole life was a romance. She was right, of course.

But where was Richard?

I had to use the ladies' room and excused myself. Finding the guest bathrooms occupied, I decided to cut through the kitchen to a little half bath near the back stairs in a hallway that led to the half dozen garages.

When I was finished, I fixed my makeup and hair and stuffed my lipstick and comb back into my black beaded purse. When I stepped out of the room, I heard voices, familiar voices: Richard's and Ashley's voices.

"Ash, don't—let's go back and dance."

"Let's dance here."

I turned a corner and saw them on the stairs, the service stairs, Uncle Lanny called them. He was an imperialist to his little white toes. Richard was backed against the wall, and Ashley had her arms about his neck, her whole body leaning into him. Let me try again—her whole body *mashed, crushed, pasted, squashed, smashed* against his. One knee curved against his leg.

Richard's hands were on her elbows. "Listen, *Ash*."

Her mouth clamped his, but his hands pushed against her elbows. I saw it clearly—he was not engaged in this kiss. He had not initiated any of this. I knew that.

I held my breath.

Ashley's knee rose on his leg. Richard pulled down on her elbows. I couldn't move, couldn't look away. I wish I could have disappeared, because then I wouldn't have seen him give in. I wouldn't have seen his arms folding around her bare back—wouldn't have seen him step forward. "He clasped her body tightly to his" is how *The Romance Writer's Phrase Book* would put it, but it's not so romantic when it's your boyfriend you're describing in a heated embrace with a girl who was once your friend.

Even now, a cold knot forms in my stomach as I write about it. It still stuns and sickens me to repeat the experience on these pages.

I dropped my purse onto the tile floor. I looked down. The clasp had opened, the lipstick rolled and stopped. I looked up.

A shadow of shock crossed Richard's face when he saw me. He pushed Ashley away. "Kate!" His voice was hoarse. Kissing can do that.

"I'm sorry," I said. I turned and ran through the kitchen, leaving the purse and its contents on the floor.

"Kate!" Richard's voice followed me through the house.

I found Helmut with my parents, still watching the fireworks. "Please, I want to go home," I said to Helmut. "Right now, please!"

"Don't you want to watch the rest of the fireworks?" Dad asked, his face turned toward the sky. "I enjoy watching Lanny's money go up in smoke."

"No. I want to go home *now*," I said with such vehemence that all three of them stared at me in surprise. I lowered my voice. "Please," I pleaded. I was afraid of weakening, afraid my chin, my lips would quiver.

Richard caught me from behind. "Kate, let me explain—" His face looked wretched, gray.

"Drop dead," I said evenly. I pulled my arm out of his grasp and headed for the coatroom, hoping Helmut would follow.

Instead Richard stayed at my heels. "Kate, please don't leave this way." His fingers grasped my arm. I pried them loose.

"Don't touch me," I said through my teeth. "Don't follow me and don't talk to me!" And then I did something that shames me even now; I slugged him as hard

160

as I could across the shoulder with a closed fist. Wearing my black velvet party dress, I slugged Richard. I slugged him hard. Helmut saw it. The man holding my coat saw it. Maybe a few other people as well. I slugged Richard with all my strength. I wanted to kill him.

He teetered a little and then backed away. "Okay," he said, his hands up in a gesture of truce. "Not here, not now."

"Not ever!" I said and walked out the front door without my coat.

Without any manipulation on my part, this chapter, filled with disappointment and suffering, turns out to be the unlucky Chapter Thirteen. It's so appropriate, and I'm pleased with this artistic coincidence, one of life's tiny miracles.

It is another of life's tiny miracles that Helmut and I remain friends to this day. He drove while I cried silently. His voice, kind and soothing, began telling me how American jokes did not translate well into German and vice versa. "For example," he said, keeping his voice very light, "take the knock-knock jokes—"

I don't know if the noise I made was an attempt to laugh or just a sob. His cowlick was now standing straight up. Even when I'm wretched, details do not escape me.

Helmut continued a soft chatter, moving from knock-knock jokes to Max and Moritz cartoons, until we stopped in my driveway.

I opened the car door. "Thank you. I'm sorry," I said.

He shrugged off the apology. "I will see you in school. Good-bye."

On the front hall table lay the Polaroid pictures my mother had taken earlier. Helmut and I, Richard and I, Richard and Helmut, and then all three of us. I went into the kitchen, pulled the scissors out of a drawer, and cut Richard out of the three pictures. Just snipped his betraying body into slivers, which I left scattered on the table.

Then I went to bed, but not to sleep. I didn't even bother taking off my glasses. I just lay on my side and looked out to the street, to Midgely's house, which was dark. He was still clinging to life in the hospital. I cried for him, but mainly for myself.

The others came home about twenty minutes later. There were no nightcaps. All of them came straight upstairs, said weary good-nights to each other, and separated into their bedrooms.

I heard Richard in the bathroom. The toilet flushed; the water ran in the basin. Then he showered, which seemed odd. The shower shut off. He went into his bedroom, leaving the bathroom light on. Jerk.

A few minutes later he was back. "Kate," he called softly from behind the door.

I stopped breathing.

"Kate? At least let me apologize. Kate?"

Roast in hell, I thought. Eat rocks.

The bathroom light clicked off.

In the morning I awoke to hear Bjorn giving Richard advice: "Just talk to her." They were out in the hallway, their voices low.

"She doesn't want to talk to me. I don't blame her, frankly."

"Send her roses; that always works." Not exactly a surprise suggestion, coming from Bjorn.

"Roses?" Richard's voice was full of disgust. "Roses won't cut it with Kate. She'll bite the blooms off and return the stems."

"I don't know. Roses always work for me—"

Their voices grew fainter as they walked toward the stairs. "Roses would make her even madder" was the last thing I heard Richard say.

You got that right, Buster.

I could not imagine sitting with Richard at the same breakfast table, could not imagine feigning civility toward him. I couldn't even think of him without seeing him and Ashley welded together. I knew what it felt like to be welded to Richard. I was not willing to share it.

Tomorrow morning, early, they would all leave in Richard's Volvo station wagon: back to Palo Alto. Back to school. I would hole up in my room until then. I went into Mother's bedroom and took the five-inch black-and-white TV set from her nightstand and carried it into my room, locking the doors. I plugged in the TV and got back into bed. The Rose Bowl Parade was on one station and the Orange Bowl Parade was on another. Very boring on colored TV, but absolutely dorky on black-and-white. I switched channels and decided on *Sesame Street* on the public station. When Kermit the Frog appeared as a journalist, I began to cry over Jim Henson's death. Kermit the Frog was dead. Ernie was dead. I sobbed out loud.

Someone knocked at the door. "Kate?" It was Mother. I unlocked the door. "Oh, Kate," she said when she saw my face. She carried a tray with muffins and jam and orange juice, which she set on my bed.

We stood in the middle of the room, my mother and I. She with her arms around me, and me sobbing, "Why did Kermit the Frog have to die? Why couldn't it have been Pee Wee Herman?"

Mother laughed then and led me to the other bed. "This is about Rich, isn't it?"

"I don't want to talk about it."

"You don't have to; I can guess. I saw what was going on." She looked down at her nails. "Looking good is the best revenge," she said.

"I don't want to see him. I don't want to see anyone."

She patted my knee. "Okay." She stood up. "Eat some breakfast and cry about Jim Henson." She smiled. When she reached the door, she turned. "I'll make excuses for you downstairs. Do you want anything else?"

I shook my head. "Thanks," I said.

"I'll check on you later," she said and disappeared.

I sat on my bed. I was pouting and withdrawing. I knew that. But when I thought of Richard, I felt only a hot anger. I began to feel more sympathy for Trish, and for Othello too. I didn't want to make up. I wanted Richard dead.

After breakfast, after a long bath, after dressing up in the world's most sensational bulky sweater and wool flannel slacks, after painting myself with blush and, yes, even lip gloss, I went downstairs and joined the others, who were watching the first of a series of football games in the living room. "Hi," I said.

"Cute sweater," Trish said. She was at the card table working on the million-piece puzzle. I sat with her.

For the rest of the day I interacted with everyone but Richard. My voice was light. I made jokes about my dad, who snoozed through most of every football game. I did an imitation of Bjorn stammering through his own wedding ceremony; I found puzzle pieces that Trish had been searching for all week, but I would not look at Richard, whom I hated with an intensity that even I couldn't believe.

Only at night, coming out of the basement with folded laundry, did I meet him face-to-face in the back hall.

"Can't we talk?" he asked.

What did I ever find attractive about him? I wondered. I moved past him. "No," I said. "I'll be glad when you're out of this house and out of my life."

In bed I thought about Jim Henson, about Midgely, about the day Ruffy got hit by a car right in front of the house a few years ago, and I bawled.

EITHER I HADN'T set my alarm, or it didn't go off. It was Mother who woke me. "They're all ready to go," she said. "Come and say good-bye."

I got up, brushed my teeth, splashed water on my face, and went downstairs. They really were ready, all of them standing outside in front of the Volvo with its motor running. Their hot breaths clouded the morning air. I threw on boots and a parka and stepped out. Mother and Dad watched while I hugged Bjorn. "Love you, Boo," he said.

"Love you too." Tears welled. We would never live in the same house again, my brother and I. I hugged him tighter. I hugged Trish too. "I love you," I said. "Sis." We both laughed, or cried. I'm not sure which. Then I stepped back in line with my parents.

Richard stood, his hands in his pockets, and stared only at me. I could not escape his gaze. "Are you going to let me apologize for hurting you?" he asked. His voice was steady, assertive. He had lost the air of the pathetic lover.

"What you do is your business," I said.

"This is *our* business." He glared.

I was faintly aware that the others were all shifting nervously back and forth on their feet.

"There is no 'our' business," I said. "There is no plural possessive adjective 'our' where you're concerned."

His eyes bored into mine until I had to look away. I shivered.

Richard handed Bjorn the keys to the Volvo. "Here," he said. "I'm not going."

"What?" Bjorn's head jerked.

"I'm not going."

"It's your car. You'll be late for school."

"Go." He opened the door for Trish and kissed her cheek as she got into the passenger seat.

"Are you sure?" Bjorn's feet seemed frozen to the driveway.

"Positive. Can I borrow your sleeping bag, the good one?"

Bjorn moved around the car, looking puzzled. He nodded. "You know where it is." He stopped. "Rich, we can wait—"

"No, I'm staying."

"What colossal dramatics!" My voice was shrill. "You can't stay here! You can't stay in my house another five minutes. Don't even try!"

"Kate!" Mother's face drained of all color. "Rich, I'm sorry—"

"She didn't mean it," Dad said, but he looked at me as if he wasn't sure.

"I'm leaving if he stays, and that's it!" My voice had a strange hysterical ring to it. I stomped toward the house.

"Kate!" My mother, I could tell, was appalled.

"It's okay," Richard said to my parents. To me he shouted, "Relax, Bjorkman, I'm not staying in your house." He turned back to my parents. "If you'd get me Bjorn's sleeping bag and a shovel, I'll be on my way."

I sneered and stormed into the house. There was coffee brewing, and I poured myself a cup and sat at the kitchen table, quietly raging. What did he think he was doing? What game was he up to now? An image of Richard's arms curved tightly around Ashley's bare back flashed in my head. Whatever game it was, I wasn't going to buy it. Not a second time. Not ever.

Mother and Dad had followed me into the house. Dad went upstairs, but Mother came into the kitchen and began putting food into an old backpack of Bjorn's.

She poured the rest of the coffee into a thermos and stuck that in there too.

I was incredulous. "You're not packing a lunch for him, are you? Can't you see he's just manipulating our whole family? Let him get his own food. Let him eat squirrel! Better yet, let him starve!" I had stood up for more effective ranting.

Mother turned, her jaw set in a way I rarely saw. "You just calm down," she said in her most authoritative voice. "If you think I'm going to let one of my best friends' son leave here on foot without anything to eat, well, then, you have another think coming." She folded napkins into the pack and began closing it up.

"You're taking his side? What about me? What about my feelings? You never support me. You never listen." I had never made a speech like this before, probably because it wasn't true, but there I was shouting it. It felt thrilling, to tell you the truth.

Mother looked up from her project. "If we haven't listened, it's because you haven't exactly been talking, have you?" Her voice was crisp but low. "You seem to prefer suffering in silence like some soap-opera queen." She turned. "Which is why problems get resolved so slowly on soaps." She had closed the backpack and set it on the table.

I thumped my cup onto the table's surface, spilling coffee. "I can't believe you're taking his side. He's the one playing games, hanging around, asking for shovels and sleeping bags with those great big cow eyes of his—"

Mother wiped at my coffee spill as if it were an obscenity. "He'd be gone if you had talked to him."

I was stampeding around the kitchen now, my boots thumping heavily against the tile. "Me, me, me! Like it's all my fault. Like I'm the one who betrayed everyone in sight! Nobody cares what I'm going through!"

"I do care what you're going through." The edge in Mother's voice was gone. "I do." She picked up the pack. "But I care about Rich too." She headed out the back door.

That did it. I grabbed my parka from the back of the chair and followed her out of the house, passed her, and made my way down the street, since none of the sidewalks were shoveled.

"Where are you going?" Mother stood next to Richard. He was holding the backpack now.

I turned. "Since you've given him all the food in the house, I'll have my breakfast at Bridgeman's, thank you very much."

That was me, Kate Bjorkman, a potential Ph.D. candidate, a fairly rational young woman—that's what my dad always said, even-tempered: "If I could only have one daughter, then Kate was the perfect one to have," he'd say. And my mother agreed. The only bad thing about me was my eyes: blind as Milton without those glasses. But that morning, January 2, I was deranged. I knew it, I guess, but I couldn't stop it. Didn't want to. It wasn't until I sat in a booth at Bridgeman's that I realized I was wearing flannel pajamas and I had no money.

THE HOUSE WAS quiet when I returned, except for the soft strains of Samuel Barber's *Adagio for Strings,* wafting from

170

Dad's study. It's one of those bittersweet pieces. Paranoid as I was, I wondered if Dad had put it on when he saw me coming.

I went up and sat for an hour in a hot bath and got dressed. When I came downstairs, Mother was in the front hall dressed for work. She searched through her handbag as she spoke. "I have to go into the office today. I'd like you to take down the Christmas tree, if you wouldn't mind. The boxes for the ornaments are downstairs."

I nodded listlessly.

"See you tonight," she said, pulling on her gloves. Our eyes avoided each other. "I'm going, Nels," she called to my dad.

"See ya tonight, babes," he called back.

Her lips turned up at the corners. Fleur was right. They were still in love. I couldn't stay in love for a week. Depressing.

It took a couple of hours to clear away the tree and vacuum up the needles. I took down the one on the piano too, took down the wreath from the dining room table; the holly and the mistletoe, all dried and curled, fell in broken scraps onto the floor. I allowed time, like a ribbon, to curve back on itself to Christmas Eve and saw Richard's face close to mine. He had used my name for the first time. "Merry Christmas, Kate," he had said. He had kissed me lightly on the lips, not once but twice. Had that been real? Had Christmas morning on the ice been real? I filtered back through the whole week, the whole precious week. And then Ashley. I tried to press down the gnawing emotion that hovered and coiled in my stomach. What was real? What was true?

When I was finished, I went to sit in Dad's study and listen to *Faustus*, an opera in which the hero gets slaughtered by devils in the end. Perfect.

That's when I saw Richard out the window that faced the back. I stood in front of it. "What is he doing?" I asked.

My dad, hunched over his computer, looked up at me and then out the window at Richard, who was shoveling snow on a mound already five feet high and several feet long.

"I'm not sure," Dad mused, "but I think he's building himself a snow cave."

I stared. Richard shoveled with an intense, steady rhythm, the hood of his parka thrown back, his breath a floating cloud of steam in front of his face. He never looked up.

"A snow cave." I was trying to recall.

"He and Bjorn made them when they were Scouts— remember?"

I didn't.

"They're supposed to keep you from freezing to death when you're caught in below-freezing temperatures."

"You mean he's going to *live* out there?" I looked at my father.

He shrugged. "Don't know, but it sure looks like it."

"Well," I said, collecting myself. "Maybe he'll freeze to death."

Dad gazed out at Richard. "I think that may be a real

possibility," he muttered, turning back to his computer. "I wouldn't spend five minutes in one of those things."

It irritated me that Richard was visible from all the south windows of the house, that I couldn't escape his presence. "Can't we make him get off our property?" I asked Dad.

He looked at me wearily. "Technically, he's not on our property. He's on the common, but"—he looked over his reading glasses at me—"even if he were, Kate, I wouldn't bother. I'm too old for these confrontations."

"Suit yourself," I said. I left to find a place to sit on the north side of the house. I worked on the puzzle, which was nearly done except for a couple of dozen stubborn pieces. It was hard to concentrate. I went upstairs and stood in my bedroom waiting for inspiration. None came. I crossed the hall to Bjorn's room and stood back from the window. Richard was scooping out the center of the snow cave, using the shovel, sometimes his hands, sometimes his feet, kicking aside clods of snow. Two squirrels scurried along a branch over his head, paused to watch him, and then scrambled up the trunk of the tree. I moved closer to the window, my warm breath forming icy patterns on the pane. I tried to wipe them away with my fingers, and when I looked down again, Richard stood leaning on the shovel, looking at me, his chest heaving from exertion. My hand was still on the glass. Across the shadowed snow of the backyard, our eyes held. Nobody smiled. It seemed like hours. Then he returned to his shoveling.

I went to the Video Mart and checked out three movies that I hoped would relieve me of the utter sense of loss I felt. The first one, which I watched before dinner, was a Stephen King horror movie in which a three-year-old returns from the dead to kill his mother and everyone else in sight. It had my complete attention, believe me.

After that I ate dinner with my parents, Mother chatting brightly about a new client she had from White Bear Lake, a Mrs. Duvander, who had one leg shorter than the other. Outside, it was already dark. When I carried my dishes to the sink, I stole a glance across the backyard. An impoverished light glowed dimly from the front of the snow cave. Some kind of lantern, I supposed. I watched the news with my parents, interested mostly in the weather report. Eighteen degrees below zero. That was the night's forecast. None of us looked at each other.

I watched another horror movie, about a man who ate his victims after murdering them, biting their faces off in some cases. "I'm having an old friend for dinner" was the last line of the movie. Finally I watched a vampire movie in which young, nubile things with white boobs bursting from lacy lingerie had the blood sucked from their necks by a really evil-looking vampire. The young nubile things all reminded me of Ashley. I enjoyed it when they died, when their eyes rolled back into their heads and they sighed their last breaths. "Die, slut, die!" I said aloud just as my mother passed by.

Her eyebrows arched.

"Not you," I said. "Her," and pointed to the brunette victim in the throes of a death rattle.

Without comment my mother passed into the study.

We watched the news again at ten. It was now twelve below zero but would get lower. After the news Bjorn and Trish called from Nebraska. I said hi to them from the extension. They wanted to know about Richard. Dad told them he was in the snow cave out in back. "The temperature is supposed to stay just above thirty-two degrees in those things, isn't it?" he asked.

Bjorn's voice sounded annoyed. "That's the theory. I don't personally know anyone who's tested one, do you?"

"Actually"—Dad cleared his throat—"no."

I clicked the extension down and wished I had another horror movie to watch.

In bed, I couldn't sleep. I kept thinking of this story called "The Dead," by James Joyce, that Midgely had us read. In it the wife tells her husband of a young lover of hers, who years earlier had stood in front of her house, looking up at her window while it snowed. Had he died of exposure? Had he frozen to death? I couldn't remember. I only remembered that the falling snow was a heavy-duty symbol in that story. Well, I thought, pulling the quilt over my head, dramatic things like that only happen in fiction. I didn't know anyone who had frozen to death ever.

Except the Hutchinses. Wendy Hutchins had been a girl in my class in fifth grade and had let me borrow her colored pencils once when we were coloring the different countries of South America and I had left my pencils at home. She and her family had pulled to the side of the highway in a blizzard and they had all frozen to death.

175

Her mother, her father, her baby brother, and her grand-mother. It had been all over the TV.

But I didn't know anyone else. Yet.

After tossing and turning for who knows how long, I got up and went into Bjorn's room across the hall and gazed out the window. The lantern was out. The snow cave, a deep purple mound, was barely visible with the trees of the common behind it. I curled up in a fetal position on Bjorn's bed, under the quilt that lay at the foot, and tried to concentrate on cannibal killers.

When I awoke, late, I knew I could not stay in my house as long as Richard lived in a snow cave out in my backyard, and I decided to spend the rest of the Christ-mas holiday at Aunt Eve's. Without looking out the win-dow, I went to the bathroom and then hurried down-stairs in my flannel nightgown. I'd announce my plans to my parents and leave.

They both stood by the sink, their backs to me, their faces leaning toward the window. I thought I heard Dad chuckle. I moved across the room next to Mother and looked out to the snow cave. Richard, alive, stood in full winter gear, holding a large sign with red printing on it. I squinted to focus my eyes on the words: WILL WORK FOR FOOD.

Something hard and tight in my chest dissolved. "Richard," I whispered aloud. "He's an idiot." A warm feeling rose in me for the first time in two days, making my chin quiver.

Mother handed me my parka. "Talk," she said.

I pulled on my fruit boots in the back hall and opened the door. The shock of the cold air pressed the tears from my eyes. I clamped my teeth shut to keep them from chattering.

When Richard saw me, he let the sign fall to the ground. We stood facing each other, he with his hands in his pockets, me with arms folded tightly across my chest. I was shuddering.

"You're crazy," I said, my chin wobbling, my nose running.

"I was a fool," he said, his eyes riveted on mine.

I nodded. "You hurt me," I said. Saying it aloud made my nose run more.

"I know, and I'm sorry—very sorry." He looked down at his feet and up again. "I don't have an excuse. I did it, because at that moment, I wanted to. I wish I hadn't."

"I trusted you." I couldn't control my stupid chin.

"I've never been so sorry about anything in my life." His voice was strained. "If I could take it back, if I could erase the whole thing, I would." He took a half-step forward. "Kate?"

I wiped my nose on my mitten.

"Are you ever going to forgive me, Kate?"

I think I nodded. I meant to. I wanted to. I think I nodded and said, "I want to."

In any case, *The Romance Writer's Phrase Book* is filled with emotion-laden descriptions of what happened next: I mean there really was "an undeniable magnetism building" between us. A magnetism neither of us could resist any longer, and we were "swept," yes, "swept" into each other's arms. I don't think that's overstating it—two clinging steel-belted radial tires in that Minnesota landscape. Richard kissed my face and said he loved me more than anybody in the whole world, which was exactly what I wanted to hear. He even "swung me in the circle of his arms," all six feet of me, and get this, "his mouth covered mine hungrily."

Yes, hungrily. And I, dear romance readers, "drank in the sweetness of his kiss."

Revision Notes

Should I just let this romance novel be as I've written it? Richard charms me out of my anger and we melt into each other? The end? Should I not tell about lying in bed that same night and realizing that making a snow cave and a sign, WILL WORK FOR FOOD, was the same as stepping into a bathtub fully clothed, which in turn was the same as sending a dozen roses? Bribery, Fleur called it. Richard himself had called it that. Grand gestures of apology, all of them—but without discussion, nothing was solved.

Should I tell about those discussions with Richard that still continue? How I now know that he has had two serious girlfriends (Karen Holden and Abby Creer) while I, foolishly, lived in a fantasy world of Richard. One-and-Only. What has hurt me is knowing that I too wanted to be a One-and-Only, and it's already too late. I'm a nineties kind of girl—only the wrong century.

And should I say anything about listening to his voice, so low and smooth, and thinking *Is this Mr. Radio speaking?* I've thought of asking Fleur again what exactly she meant by that nickname, but I'm not sure I really want to hear the answer. Not right now.

I began writing this novel thinking it would be a kick, and it has been, really, but it's also reminded me how easy romance is and how hard (this will sound corny as hell) building a real relationship is. And then too I've found that my biggest supporters aren't entirely happy with me. For example, Shannon read the whole novel yesterday and called me on the phone to say that she really liked it, but I could tell she was holding something back, so I said, "But?"

"I wish I were in your novel more." It came out in a spurt of breath. "You do a lot more things with me than you've ever done with Ashley, and I'm hardly in it."

"But the whole story takes place at Christmas and you weren't even here—"

"I know, I know, but if I'd been here, you would have been calling me on the phone all the time and I would have been at your house hanging around like I do—"

"I just wrote it like it happened," I said.

"I know," she said, "but you're calling it a novel and that's fiction. Couldn't you pretend I was home and write me into it? You know, use your imagination." Sigh.

My parents weren't any better. Mother read the novel a few days ago in the living room and said, laying the manuscript in her lap, "Is this the way you think I sound? You make me sound old."

"I do?" I had only tried to copy the way she talked.

"Except for that section where you have me telling about the fight with your dad—I wish you'd take that out. I come off so foolish."

"But that's the way you always tell it!"

"Well," she said, "I wouldn't have if I'd known you were recording every word and gesture in your brain." She had rolled the manuscript into a loaf and was squeezing it.

"The point was to show you in a weak moment, be-cause—"

"If I wanted to be shown in a weak moment, I'd call a press conference and show them the scar from my hysterec-tomy! And don't quote me!"

My dad said, "All you have me do in this novel is sleep and lust after Fleur. I seem to be a cross between Rip Van Winkle and Woody Allen."

I'm sure Ashley wouldn't like the way she's portrayed either, but I'm not letting her read it. We haven't spoken to each other since New Year's Eve, and I like it that way.

Anyway, being a writer is hard. Now I have to go through the book again and decide which of the revisions to integrate into the text and which to drop.

I know even as I write this that I won't include all this retching in the novel. Reality is not appropriate to the genre. I just read a couple of Harlequins, and I've got to edit out some of the reality in this novel as it is. I'll have to cut Midgely and the cancer (he died three weeks ago). I won't say any-thing about Richard receiving an early acceptance into the University of Minnesota's American Studies Program with a full fellowship, while I have applied to Columbia and do not expect to be turned down. Even if Richard and I marry down the line and have 2.5 children—a real possibility—I need to find out first who Kate Bjorkman is.

I'll end the novel with a happy epilogue that romance readers will adore. I promised them a happy ending, after all. And it's mostly true.

Epilogue

For the past several nights, I've been reading this romance novel I've written to Richard, on the phone. Mostly he laughs and says the book is a riot.

"This is no laughing matter," I say. "This is the story of our romance. This is serious business!"

"Right," he says. "In that case"—and he lowers his voice—"I just want to say how much I'd like to gather the soft curves of your body and mold them to the contours of my lean body."

"Now you're talking," I say. "And I want to bury my face against the corded muscles of your chest."

"You're much too tall for that," he says. "You'll have to bury your face in my nose, Amazon woman."

"Well," I say. "That sends the passion pounding through my heart, chest, and head."

"Seriously," he says. And I wonder what delicious thing he might say to me that isn't a cliché. "You ought to try having the book published."

Bingo!

"It doesn't have an ending," I say. "Category romances need a committed ending."

He snorts. "The heroine is a bit of a flake, but I know the hero is committed to her. His greedy mouth wants to open her lips and plunder the warm moistness within."

We break up laughing.

"See you in a few days, Kate."

"See you," I say.

I'm going to San Francisco over spring break. If this were one of those really sensual novels, Richard and I would hole up in a hotel room for a week, but I began the novel as a virgin and will end it as a virgin. I'm staying with his parents, Caroline and Roy. Richard and I will eat dim sum in Chinatown and I will try the duck feet, which Richard says are delicious once you get past the *idea* of duck feet. We will also eat Ghirardelli chocolates, take the boat to Alcatraz, explore the wharf, dance at the Top of the Mark, and ride the trolley to Golden Gate Park.

Later, maybe we'll marry and have a girl named Fleur and a boy named Chuck. Maybe not. One thing I know is that there will always be something to laugh about, and laughter, as it turns out, is the best aphrodisiac of all.

Printed in the United States
90087LV00002B/88/A